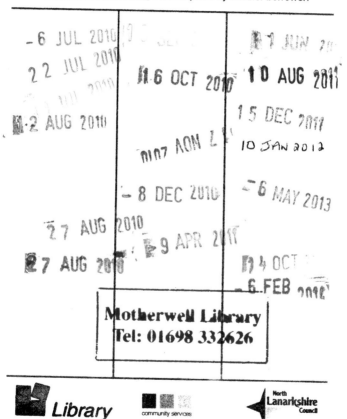

Gemma groaned in protest at the kiss ending too soon, and looked up into Stefano's eyes.

Suddenly she was all too aware of standing in his embrace, her breasts pressed to his chest, her belly flush with the flat planes of his abdomen, and the hard evidence of his desire.

She scrambled out of his reach, hating his assumption that she was his for the taking now. Hating herself even more for letting this situation spiral out of control.

He was a playboy, arrogantly sure of his prowess. He was rich and sought-after and likely believed every woman he met would gladly crawl into his bed. She certainly didn't want to feel this burning pull toward him, but she couldn't squash it either.

Yes, the sooner they got this business over with, the sooner she and Stefano could settle into a suitable work arrangement as secretary and boss.

For as long as **Janette Kenny** can remember, plots and characters have taken up residence in her head. Her parents, both voracious readers, read her the classics when she was a child. That gave birth to a deep love for literature, and allowed her to travel to exotic locales—those found between the covers of books. Janette's artist mother encouraged her yen to write. As an adolescent she began creating cartoons featuring her dad as the hero, with plots that focused on the misadventures on their family farm, and she stuffed them in the nightly newspaper for him to find. To her frustration, her sketches paled in comparison with her captions.

Her first real writing began with fan fiction, taking favourite TV shows and writing episodes and endings she loved—happily ever after, of course. In her junior year of high school she told her literature teacher she intended to write for a living one day. His advice? Pursue the dream, but don't quit the day-job.

Though she dabbled with articles, she didn't fully embrace her dream to write novels until years later, when she was a busy cosmetologist making a name for herself in her own salon. That was when she decided to write the type of stories she'd been reading—romances.

Once the writing bug bit, an incurable passion consumed her to create stories and people them. Still, it was seven more years and that many novels before she saw her first historical romance published. Now that she's also writing contemporary romances for Mills & Boon®, she finally knows that a full-time career in writing is closer to reality.

Janette shares her home and free time with a chow-shepherd mix pup she rescued from the pound, who aspires to be a lap dog. She invites you to visit her website at www.jankenny.com. She loves to hear from readers—e-mail her at janette@jankenny.com

INNOCENT IN THE ITALIAN'S POSSESSION

BY
JANETTE KENNY

MILLS & BOON

First published in Great Britain 2010
Harlequin Mills & Boon Limited,
Eton House, 18-24 Paradise Road, Richmond, Surrey TW9 1SR

© Janette Kenny 2010

ISBN: 978 0 263 21360 7

Harlequin Mills & Boon policy is to use papers that are natural, renewable and recyclable products and made from wood grown in sustainable forests. The logging and manufacturing process conform to the legal environmental regulations of the country of origin.

Printed and bound in Great Britain
by CPI Antony Rowe, Chippenham, Wiltshire

INNOCENT IN
THE ITALIAN'S
POSSESSION

CHAPTER ONE

GEMMA CARDONE hurried down the hall toward the executive suite of Marinetti Shipyard, heart pounding and nerves snapping like a ship's sails. Church bells chimed six times, the distant echo clear in the quiet Tuscan morning.

Since the day she'd come to work in Viareggio nine months ago, she'd relished her leisurely morning walk to her office. Even inside the old building, the tall narrow windows reminded her of the arched portals of the stone train tunnel along Cinque Terre, giving a teasing glimpse of endless sky, the Ligurian Sea and the rugged cliffs that crashed into the water.

In the ancient village of Manarolo where she had been born and raised, the old-world buildings scrambled up the steep rocky cliffs as if clinging to the stone face like colorful gems.

On the same rugged cliffs grew the most magnificent grapes used to make a wine found nowhere else.

It was small and remote and older than time. Everywhere there were steps and narrow lanes. Yet she missed it dreadfully at times, for there was a peace there she'd never found anywhere else.

It was just the opposite here in Viareggio. It was close to Cinque Terre by sea, yet a world apart with a festive carnival and scores of ships and industry and more tourists than she'd ever seen in a season.

This seaside coastal town stretched along the endless sandy beaches, meeting the water in a gentle slope. The architecture was pure art nouveau and the pulse of the town was upbeat.

Every day she looked forward to coming to work for Cesare Marinetti at his shipyard. But not today.

Just one week ago a tragic accident had taken the life of Cesare's wife and landed him in the hospital. Marinetti Shipyard had been shut down ever since, in mourning for Signora Marinetti and out of respect for the family.

Gemma had been on pins and needles since the funeral, worried sick about the heart attack that had kept Cesare hospitalized. It was no small wonder that the employees wondered when Cesare would be able to resume control of his shipyard. Until then, who would manage it in his stead?

The answer had come in the wee hours of the morning.

"I do not have long to talk," Cesare had rasped in a voice clearly laced with pain. "The doctors say I need heart bypass surgery, and I believe them." His sigh was long and weary, like one resigned to his fate. "The shipyard will open today, but I will not return to work for weeks."

"Of course," she said, her heart heavy over what he'd be facing with surgery and recuperation while still burdened with grief over losing his wife. "Who are you placing in charge of Marinetti?"

A thick curse rumbled over the line. "My son is taking over the shipyard."

No! Cesare had called in the son who'd turned his back on him five years ago? The one who never called, never visited because he was too busy playing the part of consummate playboy?

"I confessed all, Gemma, now I live to regret it. You must go to the office immediately and remove all the documents pertaining to my daughter and you," he said. "Take them home with you and keep them hidden. I cannot let the truth be known yet, not at this point and especially not to Stefano."

Of course, Cesare was right. If his secret was made public now, it would rock Marinetti Shipyard and cause his family more hurt. She didn't want to guess what undue grief it would bring his daughter in her fragile condition.

"Don't worry," she said. "I'll take care of things."

"*Grazie*! Be careful around Stefano and don't let him know when you intend to travel to Milan."

That warning played over and over in her mind as she hurried down the Promenade toward the shipyard. The bars, shops and cafés still slept, but it wouldn't be long and the town would come awake. What other surprises would this day bring?

She hated to guess as she made her way toward the executive suite on the upper floor of Marinetti Shipyard. The heels on her Italian sandals tapped the wooden floor with an urgent beat that kept pace with her heart.

She simply couldn't fail Cesare in this. Not now. Not after all they'd been through together.

The click of a door closing echoed up the stairwell just as she reached the end of the hall. She whipped around and went still as death, looking, listening.

Unease arched between her shoulder blades as a tense quiet hummed around her. She saw no one about. But a door had closed in the stairwell below. She was certain of it.

None of the office staff should be here yet. In fact there was no reason for any employee to come to work over an hour early. No *good* reason, that is.

It must be the security guard making his rounds. Yes, it must be.

Still, Gemma all but ran the last few meters to the paneled door of her office. She couldn't get caught by anyone. That would raise questions she wasn't prepared to answer, and she never had been able to tell a convincing lie.

She hurried into her small office painted cheery yellow and furnished with an efficient desk and chair, a quartet of padded chairs along the wall for guests, and a table arranged with a lamp and several magazines. Sunlight streamed through the window in a burst of welcome, but pausing to appreciate its beauty would have to wait.

She pushed into Cesare's office and flipped the wall switch with a shaking finger. Before the soft light could chase the shadows to the dark corners of the paneled room, she was heading across the maroon and jade carpet toward the wall safe.

Despite the cool morning, sweat beaded her forehead and dampened her spine and palms. Her silk coral blouse clung to her breasts and her navy blue pencil skirt had ridden up her thighs from her uncharacteristic sprint. But she couldn't take time to right her clothes, either.

An unsettling energy hummed in the air, as if a storm was moving in. Or trouble was brewing?

Please don't let it be from within Marinetti.

They'd all been through enough. But she feared that's just what would happen when Cesare's son took over.

From what she'd overheard, Stefano Marinetti was ruthless in business and a lothario outside of it. Having seen him at the funeral, she didn't doubt that rumor one bit!

Yes, he was praised for his rapier-quick decisions and ability to make millions. But he was an international playboy.

He hadn't taken time to visit his parents in five long years. In her opinion, he could just stay away now.

Just recalling the latest headline splashed across the tabloids had her pursing her lips. Stefano's superyacht business had skyrocketed while Marinetti Shipyard struggled from week to week to make payroll of late.

Cesare's business rivals called him washed up. She knew the truth, but she couldn't divulge where the fortune had gone.

She spun the dial on the safe with trembling fingers, the only sound in the room her pounding heart and the metered tick of the wall clock. Then she heard the heavy outside door snick open, but it was the masculine exchange of, "*ciao*," echoing from the hall outside her office that nearly stopped her heart.

She pawed through the contents of the safe and removed the portfolio she needed with her heart in her throat, clinging to the tiny window of time afforded her as the two men outside lapsed into a rapid staccato of conversation. A quick look inside the dark safe proved the photos were stowed there as well.

She stuffed the lot of them inside her carryall, closed the wall safe and slipped from Cesare's office into her own. Footsteps pounded in the hall, coming closer. Heavy, impatient strides.

Surely not a guard. She doubted he was a worker, either. No, in all likelihood, the man moments from bursting through the door was Cesare's son.

Her heart raced as she eased onto her chair and tucked her carryall under her desk. She'd done it. Now all she had to do was don a professional air and appear to be dutifully busy.

The door swung open and a tall man strode inside, wearing an Armani suit that emphasized the width of his broad shoulders and fitted his long lean body to perfection. He stopped cold and cut her a quick impatient look, much the same expression he'd worn at his mother's funeral.

Stefano Marinetti was a younger, more leonine version of Cesare. His wealth of coffee-brown hair had a sexy wave to it and his beautifully sculpted lips curved just enough to keep him from appearing cross.

Just like he'd done at the funeral, his discerning mocha eyes took their time caressing every inch of her until her skin tingled and her thighs trembled. Men had openly stared at her before, but never like this. Never with this open carnal hunger.

It was totally inappropriate behavior even for a flirtatious Italian. He wasn't just undressing her with his hot gaze, he was getting under her skin and stroking her libido.

With effort, she broke eye contact and struggled to draw air deeply into her too tight lungs. Another mistake, for she inhaled his scent, an erotic spice that sank into her and left her giddy with want.

She hated this electric attraction to him, yet she was drawn to him all the same. It was maddening. Humiliating. Addictive.

Her heart rate trebled from the realization she'd have to work for this playboy until Cesare returned. She couldn't do it. But she couldn't *not* do it, either.

Her promise to Cesare echoed in her mind, but it was the memory of the gamine face of the little girl smiling up at her from her hospital bed that gave Gemma the strength to meet Stefano's stare dead-on.

His presence dominated the room so completely she couldn't have looked away again if she'd tried. She'd heard of imposing forces before, but she'd never been faced with one until now.

The tabloids had been right. His classic good looks rivaled the Roman gods. Contemplative. Intense. Sexy.

And impatient.

That was the unsettling energy she'd sensed before. This man was used to giving orders and having them obeyed immediately without question.

She could easily picture him as a Roman gladiator brazenly vanquishing his rivals. Or as a god lounging by a pool with a bevy of maidens at his beck and call.

Yes, his raw masculine beauty paled in comparison to the carnal energy that emanated from him. He was a businessman who oozed sensual charisma and he knew it. He flaunted it. He used it to his advantage, just as he was doing now to throw her totally off track.

Stefano was a dangerous predator here for one reason—to usurp Cesare. She'd do well to bear that in mind.

She forced a welcoming smile and struggled for a neutral tone. "*Buongiorno*, Signor Marinetti. May I personally extend my condolences on your mother's untimely passing."

He gave an impatient nod and scanned her office as if looking for something. "Where is Donna?"

"She retired nearly a year ago."

His brows snapped together and the sculpted bow to his sensual mouth thinned. "When were you hired?"

"Nearly a year ago."

"Interesting." He treated her to another exacting perusal that left her flushed and feeling vulnerable and inadequate, which shouldn't surprise her for she certainly wasn't the type who'd appeal to this arrogant jet-setter. "You are?"

"Gemma Cardone."

One devilishly black brow arched in a universally silent order that she expound on her role here.

She kept her smile in place and counted to twenty before appeasing his curiosity. "I am Cesare's personal secretary."

No emotion showed on his classically handsome face, but

the expansive line of his shoulders snapped taut. "Are you in the habit of coming to work this early?"

"No," she said honestly, for she was certain he'd discern a lie if she attempted to voice one now.

He was simply too observant as well as overwhelming to her senses. She'd sensed his dominance—no, his arrogance—at his mother's funeral.

He'd seemed emotionless then. No, that wasn't true. He'd seemed angry, like Etna rumbling deep and threatening to spew and destroy all.

She'd never been more aware of a man as she'd been then. She'd thought it a fluke until he'd walked through the door now and took command of the relaxed offices.

He was staring at her with eyes that were hard and nearly impossible to tear her gaze from. But she sensed his silent command for her to finish her thought. His *impatient* command.

Stefano Marinetti was dangerous.

It took every ounce of fortitude she could summon forth to hold her serene smile when she felt anything but composed. "I knew there would be a surfeit of correspondence to address in regard to Cesare's heart attack and tragic loss."

He gave a curt nod as if accepting her excuse. "That is good that you've taken the initiative in this delicate and most tragic matter."

She wouldn't lie about this. "Actually Cesare asked me to draft letters to his close friends and longtime business associates."

"Cesare phoned you, then?" he asked, his voice as casual as if they were discussing the weather.

Even if she was good at weaving tales, it was too late to lie now. "Last night."

"He is on strict bed rest."

"It was a brief call," she said, absently twirling the ring on her finger then stopping when the action drew his attention. Did anything slip past him? "We talked no more than a few minutes."

"Did my father tell you to report to him daily?" he said, and this time there was no mistaking the steel ringing in his voice.

"No," she said, and then certain he'd not believe the truth, asked with as much cheek as she could inflect in her tone, "Should I?"

A ghost of a smile teased those masculine lips that undoubtedly knew how to kiss a woman senseless. "Does my father call you Gemma or Ms. Cardone?"

"Cesare prefers an informal working environment." Something Stefano would know if he hadn't turned his back on his papa and the business years ago.

His features looked carved from stone, leaving her to guess he didn't like the fact that she and his papa were on a first name basis. Fine, she was here to do all she could to help Cesare, not to please Stefano Marinetti.

Anger streaked through her as she thought of how much Cesare had needed help over the past nine months. If he'd only called on his son then. And what of Stefano? How much heartache could have been avoided if he'd been an attentive son?

Was he even aware of the financial troubles plaguing Marinetti Shipyard? Surely he'd heard the rumors. He should have contacted his papa then. He, with his boasted billions, should have offered to help his father.

But no, he'd waited until Cesare was grieving and in ill health before slithering back.

For Cesare's sake, she'd count the days until Stefano took his leave. But heavens, she suspected it would be a struggle to keep her temper and her dignity around this spoiled, arrogant man.

"Very well, Gemma," he said, her name rolling off his tongue like a caress that was so inappropriate she blushed. "As my father and I agree on this, we will continue to operate on an informal basis. Alert the department managers that I expect them in my office at two o'clock for a company meeting."

"Today?"

"Yes. Is that a problem?"

"Not at all."

Stefano walked into the office and closed the door behind him with a firm click that signaled he wished privacy until then. Fine! She wanted the same.

She desperately needed it after the rush to remove Cesare's documents followed by her first meeting with Stefano.

She dropped onto her chair, shaken and angry and so relieved that she'd have a moment's peace. But how long would it last?

Too long!

He was a handsome, virile man. A handsome, virile, *arrogant* man who was taking over and placing her in a very precarious position.

That's what she needed to concentrate on. *His* unreasonable demands. And the fact that his father hadn't trusted him with his deepest secret.

Oh, Cesare! She'd do anything for him. She'd done it already. But she'd do more.

Her unwanted attraction to Stefano had temporarily blindsided her. Nothing more. She'd be better prepared the next time she was in his company.

"*Scusi*, Gemma," he said, startling her with his nearness which came far too soon for her liking. "A moment, please."

Never mind that her name rolled off his tongue like an endearment and feathered sensual awareness up her bare arms. So much for her vow to remain unaffected by him.

She forced a calm demeanor she surely didn't feel. "What do you need?"

A smile teased his mouth which was at odds with the hot look he cast her. "Would you help me make coffee? I can never do it right."

And he thought she could? She bit back that question and the sarcastic tone that begged to be loosed. "If you wish."

"*Grazie.*"

She rose and smoothed down her skirt which had the annoying habit of creeping up her thighs. His heated gaze watched her every movement and she damned the warmth flooding her face as much as she damned the fact he had a knack for keeping her on edge. Purposely, she would bet!

Make his coffee indeed, she thought as she went about the simple task. Yes, she always prepared a pot for Cesare. She would do the same for his infuriating son from now on— before he arrived at the office.

"How do you take it?" she asked.

"*Ristretto.*"

She wasn't surprised he preferred his strong and black. But she hadn't expected his attentiveness to her every move. It was unnerving in the extreme.

"You make it look so easy," he said when she had the coffee on and the rich aroma began filling the room.

She glanced up at him and was instantly ensnared by the hot promise in his eyes. Good grief, was he flirting with her?

Of course he was. All Italian men flirted, and Stefano was reputed to be an outrageous flirt. She'd just not had the opportunity to witness it before now.

"Is there anything else you need?" she asked, aiming for a cool voice that would let him know she wasn't the least bit interested in him.

"Not at the moment," he said, though the lusty gleam in his eyes contradicted his reply.

Her spine went stiff as she left the room that seemed far too close with him in it. How dare he be so cavalier with her one moment and charismatically male the next!

He'd likely find some task to interrupt her work later. She was certain of it.

Back at her desk, she set to work contacting the department managers. Most asked when Cesare would return to work. Others expressed concerns about what would happen if Cesare was forced to retire or if he died.

The last left her with an ache in her stomach and a heaviness in her heart. It hadn't been that long ago that she'd lost her own papa in a boating accident.

She certainly didn't want to think about losing Cesare! But she was worried about him. A deep unsettling worry that would likely rob her of sleep and keep her on edge.

Some months ago, Cesare had confided in her that he and his son hadn't been on speaking terms in years. The old man didn't have to tell her that upset him. She could tell.

He loved his youngest son, but according to Cesare, Stefano had disagreed with him and his eldest son over how to run Marinetti Shipyard. So he had left the company and struck out on his own and their estrangement had remained.

Interesting that Stefano had returned and stepped into the role of CEO now. Surely he wouldn't take advantage of Cesare's illness to disrupt the way things were done here? Surely he wouldn't make drastic changes?

Her intercom buzzed, a long discordant sound that rifled the calm she'd desperately sought. So much for getting a reprieve from Stefano this morning.

She jammed a finger on the call button. "*Sì, signor.*"

"Stefano." The silken timbre of his voice stirred a restless energy in her—something that was better left sleeping around him. "I have need of your services."

"Coming."

She stood and smoothed a hand over her skirt that had crept up her thighs, picked up her pen and notepad, and marched into the lion's den. She was immediately thrust into another breathless moment of sensual awareness as her gaze locked on the sexy man lounging at Cesare's desk.

He'd removed his jacket and slung it carelessly on the leather sofa, as if settling in to work. He'd even rolled up his shirtsleeves and left his cuff links lying on the desktop, the stones glinting the fire of diamonds in the light. But he still looked more the playboy than executive.

His silk tie hung loose around the strong column of his neck. His stark white shirt was open at the collar, revealing a wedge of olive skin sprinkled with black hair.

The same dark hair sprang from his forearms that were corded with muscle. A Gucci watch banded one wrist.

Anger knotted her stomach. Everything about him screamed money and sophistication. He was the consummate billionaire flaunting an extravagance that Cesare certainly couldn't afford.

Up until nine months ago, Marinetti Shipyard had made a marginal profit building fishing boats and ferries. Some called Marinetti Shipyard antiquated.

Of late, she'd heard the rumors that it was on the verge of collapse. The last hurt the most because it was true.

Cesare had been forced to dig deeply into the profits and a failure of new orders coming in had been unable to compensate for the loss. If she could, she would've given back the money Cesare had insisted she take.

But it was gone and her only source of income now was

her salary. Without Cesare running his business, how much longer could they go on?

Just last week Cesare had confessed that he'd had to sell a good deal of his shares to Canto Di Mare in order to make payroll. He barely held controlling interest in his own company. No wonder his health had broke!

Without another word or glance Stefano's way, she settled into the chair before Cesare's desk, ready to take dictation from her temporary boss. She would surely count the days until Cesare's return.

"I will be dividing my time between Marinetti and my own company," he began, rocking back in the chair with lazy insouciance and surprising her with that announcement. "After my father's surgery, of course."

"Of course."

Good! Stefano would only be here part-time. He was likely bored already with his papa's business.

Cesare Marinetti was old school and his schedule at Marinetti Shipyard was relaxed. Everything here was done in slow precision as it had been done for generations.

Even a good many of the employees were extended family with sons following in their fathers' footsteps. But what would Stefano know of that?

He'd walked away from his family. He'd found fault with the way this shipyard was run years ago. He'd shunned tradition.

"As my own secretary is on holiday," Stefano said, snaring her attention. "You will accompany me as I commute between both locations."

Was he joking? She had no intentions of being at his beck and call, especially since she had so much to do for Cesare in Milan. That took precedence over bowing to Stefano's whims.

"That is impossible. My work is here," she said.

CHAPTER TWO

THE mouth she'd earlier admired curved into a devilish smile that sent her stomach cartwheeling. She knew before he said a word that she'd just baited the lion. And lost.

"Your work is wherever and whatever I deem it to be for the foreseeable future. And," he said, raising one finger when she opened her mouth to voice a weak objection, "to make myself clear, my father is on strict bed rest before his surgery and throughout his recuperation. That includes personal business."

Those last four words shot ice down her spine. He was ordering her to keep away from Cesare. The wall had been thrown up. It was a small wonder Cesare was able to contact her when he had. Which was likely what his son had antici-pated when he took over.

At least she'd gotten the files out in time. She'd simply have to keep them hidden until Cesare returned. And she would guard them with her life.

"Am I forbidden to visit him, as well?" she asked, worry seeping into her bones when she thought of the little girl waiting for Cesare in Milan.

They couldn't just abandon her now. If Cesare was unable to see to her care, then Gemma would have to do so for him. But first she'd have to get away from Stefano.

That could prove difficult, considering he planned to take her away from here in the capacity of *his* personal assistant.

"You may visit my father." He stroked the chiseled line of his classically strong jaw with a thumb as if carefully considering her question. "After his surgery."

If she thought he was genuinely concerned about the older man's health prior to the heart bypass, she'd not take this personally. But the hard glint in his eyes mirrored the undertone in his warning—one meant just for her. Could he know of her deep relationship with Cesare? Had he somehow discovered his papa's secret?

No, that was impossible. She and Cesare had been discreet to a fault. Cesare had doled out a fortune to ensure privacy at the hospital.

Stefano was just throwing his weight around in hopes she would make a mistake. Well, it was time she reminded him that she worked for his papa first and him second.

She got to her feet, still clutching her notepad like a shield. "Cesare wanted me to prepare a detailed list of the ships we are contracted to build during the next year. If you are through, I'd like to get started on it."

"This is to be included in the prospectus for the new stockholder?"

"Yes," she said, unsettled by the mesmerizing intensity of his eyes that seemed to look right through her.

He lifted one broad shoulder in a careless shrug. "It can wait."

"No, it can't," she shot back. "Cesare made it clear that the paperwork must be completed today."

"I am telling you it can wait."

She threw a hand in the air, disgusted that Stefano wasn't taking his papa's wishes seriously. "You may not care if your father's business flourishes or fails but I do. Until I hear otherwise, he is my boss, not you."

Gemma could have crawled under the table, for she'd never, *never*, let her emotions get the better of her until now. But Stefano Marinetti seemed to know what buttons to jab to push her over the edge. And wouldn't that be a crime!

If she walked out, Cesare would have nobody in his corner. He'd have to reveal his secret and face the consequences. And a little girl would be exposed and branded a bastard.

Her shoulders slumped, for that realization was all it took for her to pull in her claws. She'd been the object of scorn before. She certainly wouldn't wish it on another innocent. Besides, she'd given Cesare her word that she'd carry on with her role here.

"Forgive my lack of manners," she said.

He toyed with a pen, and she had the distinct feeling he thoroughly enjoyed baiting his adversaries, especially her. God knew they were on opposite sides.

She was Cesare's personal secretary and loved her job and her boss. He was estranged from his father and had made no attempt to bridge the breach. Until now, when his papa was incapacitated.

That bald fact instantly put her on the wrong side of Stefano. Was he here to help his papa, or did he have a personal agenda?

"You are a fierce champion of my father," he said.

"I am simply doing my job."

"You are doing far more than that."

She didn't delude herself into thinking he was handing out a compliment. She simply clung to the hope that he'd decide to hire a temporary secretary and release her to go about Cesare's business uninterrupted.

"You should know that I'm aware of why you refused to work for your father."

"And that reason would be?"

She lifted her chin, refusing to be cowed. "Your rivalry with your brother and your refusal to take orders from him."

He stared at her for one long, uncomfortable moment. "Did my papa tell you that?"

"Most of it," she said. "The rest I heard shortly after I came to work here."

"Gossip. Let me tell you the truth." He slammed across the office, fists clutched at his sides. "My brother's wife drove me from here."

This was getting far too personal for her liking. "Really, you don't have to explain your differences—"

"Before she married my brother, she was my lover. I thought myself in love with her, so I brought her home to meet my parents." He faced her, and the anger on his face was a terrible thing to witness. "She decided my brother was the better catch as he was the heir to the company. Davide had no compunction about sleeping with her behind my back."

No wonder he demanded loyalty and honesty from his employees. "That's why you left Marinetti Shipyard. You couldn't stand to work with your brother and be around her."

"That was the deciding reason for me to leave. There were other clashes over designs and management." His gaze met hers, and the cold finality reflected in their depths made her shiver. "Are you satisfied now?"

Shocked was more like it. "I'm sorry you were betrayed by your brother and lover."

"I don't want your pity, Miss Cardone."

He stared at her a long, uncomfortable moment, the intensity in his eyes searing through her as if branding her. Or perhaps burning her at the stake for dredging up such painful memories.

"May I go now?" she asked.

His chin dipped. "See to this list that you're determined to complete."

She turned and hurried to the door, a heartbeat away from escaping him when the deep velvet rumble of his voice ribboned around her and brought her up short.

"Bring me the portfolio when you're done," he said. "I wish to review it before handing it over to my accountant."

It wasn't so much his words as it was the assurance in his voice that filled her with dread. She turned to face him, only to find him staring at her as if he could swallow her up whole and enjoy every second.

She hiked her chin up, annoyed that she couldn't stop him from getting to her, that he could make her tremble with anger and an emotion she barely understood. He was certainly bringing out the worst in her!

"Why should your accountant review Cesare's files when we have one employed who can do the same?" she asked, holding back the burning question of why he needed to see the list in the first place. In her heart she knew it couldn't be a good reason.

"Simple, Gemma. I am the CEO and owner of Canto Di Mare."

It took a moment to process that news. When it did, her thoughts tossed between outrage and awe.

"You are the new stockholder of Marinetti?"

He dipped his arrogant head in answer. "Now if you will excuse me, I have work to do. I expect those files before you leave for the day."

She took that curt dismissal as a godsend and slipped from the room. But peace eluded her.

Stefano wasn't doing his father a favor by stepping into his shoes now. He had a vested interest in the shipyard. She trembled with annoyance and fear of what this arrogant, domineering and ruthless man intended to do.

Worry stacked on her narrow shoulders like a child's wooden blocks, weighing her down, each new burden threatening to send the whole toppling around her. The company. Cesare. His love child.

She could certainly imagine Stefano meting out vengeance with great relish. Is that why Cesare had warned her to keep his secret close to her heart? Was he afraid of what his son would do if he learned the truth?

Gemma had only one way of knowing those answers, and she simply couldn't take the risk. A child's future was at stake. If Cesare hadn't made proper provisions for her... Well, then Gemma would have to see to the child's care herself.

She'd have to mind her own errant thoughts as well regarding one arrogantly handsome Italian who commanded too much of her time and thoughts.

Stefano had controlling interest in Marinetti. She was at the mercy of a man who clearly had none to spare. No matter what, she had to stay in Stefano's good graces, for too much was at stake if she failed.

Stefano Marinetti watched the tempting secretary flounce from the office and allowed a smile of appreciation. His papa had impeccable taste in women.

Gemma was more tantalizing than most with her thick, wavy hair that was kissed with streaks of blond and her naturally fair skin that had acquired a golden tan. Her wide eyes were the same mysterious blue as the Aegean Sea. Her mouth was a perfect bow that begged a man to kiss her.

Yes, she had an Italian surname, but he would bet she had a good deal of English blood in her. Perhaps she was the daughter of an expatriate who'd come to Italy to find a rich husband. Instead that woman had gotten snared by a fisherman.

Not that Gemma's heritage made a damned bit of difference to him.

She was still doing all she could to cushion her life. Too bad the little piece of fluff had sunk her claws into his papa when the old man was at his lowest.

He shoved Gemma from his thoughts and rang up the accounting department. By now every one in Marinetti's employ would know that he'd assumed the reins of the company.

Now it was time to get down to business.

"*Buongiorno*, Umberto," Stefano said in greeting as the little man he remembered so well from childhood answered the phone.

"Stefano? *Buongiorno*," the man replied warmly, and Stefano smiled, certain the older man would have kissed his cheeks had they met in person. "It is good you are back to manage the company."

"*Sì*." Though he imagined not everyone at Marinetti would share his relief.

His papa's employees had always been loyal. To a fault? He'd soon find out.

"I am acquainting myself with my father's recent business dealings and I need your help. Last month, did my father make a substantial withdrawal of company funds?"

The riffling of papers came over the line. Papers, when the company should be solely using computers!

"*Sì*, Cesare requested an expenditure." Umberto noted the date.

Stefano set his teeth. It was the same time of month that his father and Gemma set aside for their jaunt to Milan.

"What was the purpose of this advance?"

"It wasn't my place to ask," Umberto said.

Stefano smoothed a thumb and forefinger over his brow, frustrated by the old-world attitude of his father's employees. The misappropriation of funds should have thrown up red flags to the man in charge of finances.

Stefano gave a clipped thanks and ended the call.

He'd been able to launch a swift investigation on Friday, but he'd only been able to discern one damning thing. In the past nine months, his papa had taken monthly trips to Milan with Gemma Cardone. Each time a substantial amount of funds were removed from his personal account.

Clearly any money his father gave Gemma was for services rendered in her role as his mistress. Considering the staggering amount she'd gained, she must be very good in bed!

That was a thought he didn't wish to dwell on.

Never mind that his body thrummed with sensual energy whenever she was near. She was a desirable woman and he was a red-blooded Italian who loved to love women.

That was all there was to it. That's all there would ever be! He wouldn't dally with his father's leavings, nor would he fall under the charms of a scheming gold-digger again!

He would make her regret milking his father out of a fortune and causing his mamma such heartache. He could still hear the pain and fury in her voice when she'd phoned him just a week before she died.

"I have been publicly humiliated," his mother had said. "I went shopping with your aunt Althea, only to be taken aside in the store and told that there was a block on my account!"

He could guess how her Sicilian blood must have boiled. "What did Papa say about this?"

"He told me that times were hard for the business. That he hadn't said anything earlier because he didn't wish to worry me," she said. "But that was a lie. The old fool has taken a mistress. After thirty-three years of fidelity, he suddenly decides to take a lover."

"You're sure of this?"

"Positive," she'd said. "Ever since he hired that *woman* nine months ago, he pays little attention to me."

The *woman* being Gemma Cardone with her innocent smile and seductive body. "You've based your suspicions on Papa hiring a new secretary?"

That heaped more coals on his mamma's fiery temper. "They work together all day. They go away on business trips every month, yet Cesare denies he is branching out the shipping business. So I ask you what are they doing on these trips to Milan?"

Stefano hadn't a clue, but his mother's suspicions convinced him to look into his father's affairs. It had been simple to follow his papa's treks to Milan.

Each month he and Gemma drove the same route to Milan. They always lent the same suite in the hotel. They'd hole up there for three or four days. Stolen moments. A *tryst de amore*, he was sure.

Perhaps his father needed a young woman to fire his blood and make him feel virile again. These things happened. But Stefano wouldn't tolerate his papa abusing his mother.

If Cesare Marinetti took a mistress to satisfy his lust, he must make concessions to his wife to soothe her pride.

As for Stefano, he damn sure couldn't let a gold-digger bankrupt his father's company! However, a car wreck one week ago had taken his mamma's life and had nearly done the same to his papa. There had been no time to think about righting the wrong until now.

He splayed his hands on the desk and felt his blood pounding at his fingertips. Two things topped his agenda: Get Marinetti Shipping back on track and send Gemma Cardone packing.

His muscles clenched in anger—and desire—as he thought of her seducing his papa out of so much. Too much to let her get off easy.

His papa must have been over the moon for her. And why wouldn't he?

She was more tempting than he'd imagined. Despite knowing what she was, he'd been powerless to stop the desire that had erupted inside him and flowed hotter than lava off volatile Mount Etna.

Hotter still than the Sicilian blood inherited from his mamma that demanded the satisfaction of vengeance and desire. He could hold a tight fist on his explosive anger, but he was powerless to control his desire for Gemma, and that admission angered him all the more.

No woman had ever had that much power over him. Not even the young gorgeous lover he'd brought home from college. He'd been unsure of the depth of his love for her. He'd questioned her profession of love for him.

But he hadn't realized she'd been a gold-digger until she had seduced his brother. How ironic that she'd have had more wealth had she remained with Stefano.

It was a hard lesson learned. He'd not be duped again—especially by his father's mistress!

Maledizione! She'd caused his mother untold grief, and made a fool of his papa. She'd not do the same to him.

But even as his heart thundered with the need for retribution, he knew a swift punishment wasn't enough. No, Gemma Cardone should be made to suffer as his mamma has suffered the last few weeks of her life.

He strode to the window and stared out at the shipyard that had been in his family for generations. Marinettis had made their mark in quality ships, thanks to the seafaring men of Italy and the Mediterranean. Fishermen needed boats and ports needed ferries.

Like his papa and grandpapa before him, Cesare had embraced that simple prescription for success. He saw no reason to deviate or expand.

Stefano did. He had dreams of a bigger empire. A larger, cleaner international empire.

He'd wanted to build eco-friendly vessels. Sailboats, ferries, trawlers and *d'elite* superyachts. Ships that would rule the seas yet not destroy the fragile environment.

The superyacht would be the starship of his company. Floating pleasure palaces for the ultrarich, each custom made to suit discerning tastes.

His papa thought his idea was an adulteration of the principles of the company. They had butted heads. They had argued fiercely as only Italians do.

His papa insisted they were shipbuilders for Italians. Cesare was a millionaire and was content to move in that circle, refusing to cater to the whims of the ultrarich. He expected Stefano to fall into step with him just as his brother Davide had adhered to the niche Marinetti had carved for itself.

In fact, he and his brother had clashed the hardest. Over business, and the woman who'd come between them.

Stefano couldn't or wouldn't comply, not when he was nothing more than the second son in charge of menial tasks.

Not when his papa refused to consider his ideas, preferring to adhere to the routine that he and Davide had hammered into place. Not when he had to watch his former lover's belly grow with his brother's child.

His heart hadn't been broken, but his pride had surely been kicked hard.

Stefano didn't regret leaving this old-world business mired in old-world attitudes. He'd made his fortune and continued to build on it. He'd made a name for himself. But it hurt his pride that his papa hadn't praised his business sense or his daring once in the past five years.

He rested his fists on the windowsill, the wood as unyielding as his papa. Pride and honor ran deep in his veins.

One kept him away, even after the tragic death of his brother and his family.

One brought him back.

He flicked another impatient glance at the connecting door. Marinetti Shipyard had operated the same for years, making a profit that had allowed his papa to maintain his millionaire status. But all that had changed one year ago.

That's when his papa had hired Gemma Cardone. That's when his papa had begun spending more time with her in Milan than at his shipyard. That's when thousands upon thousands of euros had vanished.

Stefano returned to the desk and lounged in the chair from which his papa had ruled for so long. He opened the file his accountant had assembled and welcomed the bite of anger nipping along his nerves.

He abhorred deceit. Gemma had smoothly deceived his papa. She deserved to be treated in kind.

He jabbed the intercom button. "Join me, Gemma. Now."

"Yes, sir." Was there a touch of annoyance in her voice?

It pleased him that she was peeved to be at his beck and call. He wanted her to finally earn her paycheck by actually working.

She stepped inside and faltered, her pen and notepad clutched tightly in hand again. "What do you want?"

Due compensation. His blood heated, his muscles tightening as his gaze slid over her curves. *You*, bella. *I want you.*

This carnal attraction to her annoyed the hell out of him. He favored sophisticated women who wanted nothing more than a physical relationship. He had neither the time nor patience to suffer manipulative women.

Never mind the fact that Gemma Cardone stared back at him with a wide-eyed vulnerability that made his mouth go dry. He had the proof that she was a schemer, out to get all she could out of his papa. She'd certainly achieved that end!

He wouldn't be surprised if she hoped to lure him into her silken trap as well. That would never happen.

She would not seduce him as she had Cesare Marinetti. It would be a waste of her time to use her wiles on him for he was immune to such machinations.

He meant to give her tempting body a dismissing look, but found himself appreciating the way her silk blouse draped over her full breasts. How her skirt nipped in at her slender waist only to flare over her womanly hips.

His muscles tensed and blood pooled in his groin just at the thought of pressing her back on his desk and making love with her. He curled his fingers into fists and pressed the knuckles into the wood, vexed that his body was still not listening to his brain where she was concerned.

Perhaps he'd be wise to sever all ties with Gemma Cardone now. He could certainly afford to replace his papa's lost fortune.

He'd be free of this temptation and could devote his attention to the shipyard.

But a swift dismissal would let her off scot-free to practice her duplicity on another victim. Word would quickly spread that Cesare and Stefano Marinetti were easy marks.

No, he had to make an example of her. He had to venerate his mamma's cry for vengeance. He couldn't let Gemma Cardone get away with such duplicity.

His gaze narrowed on the mistress who seemed too damned poised.

Sì, too much pride and honor was at stake to sweep this nasty business under the rug. He had to publicly ruin this little schemer. The sooner, the better.

Stefano waved a hand at the chair before his desk, impatient to get this unpleasantness finished. She hesitated in the doorway a heartbeat before quickly crossing the room.

His pulse began racing as his gaze lingered on the brief skirt that hugged her thighs and showcased long, elegant legs that could cling to a man's flanks as they writhed in the throes of passion. *Maledizione*! He didn't want to think of seducing her.

He damned sure didn't want to think of her doing the same to his papa. That image sent anger bolting through him with the burning intensity of a lightning strike.

Damn seductive gold-digger.

Damned beautiful gold-digger.

As soon as she was seated, he began. "I want to know what business my father and you conducted in Milan for the past nine months."

She went still as death, fixing those expressive blue eyes on him again. Her small fingers tightened around the edge of her notepad and her back stiffened, as if ready to defend something that wasn't defendable. "That is between me and your father."

"Not anymore," he said, gaining satisfaction in watching

her glare at him as if he were in the wrong—the guilty always tried to divert attention away from themselves. "I hold majority shares in Marinetti Shipyard. The profits and debts are now mine to manage."

She blinked and the steel in her spine seemed to bow, as if burdened by that news. "Are you actually taking over your papa's company?"

"My plans are not open to discussion," he said. "We were discussing your role in my father's life."

The color drained from her face. "I told you I'm his personal secretary."

He snorted. She must think him as gullible as his papa.

"Were you aware that my father is nearly bankrupt?" he said.

Her face turned as white as marble. "I—I knew he was having financial difficulties of late."

"Yet you continued to take thousands of euros from him every month, even though he could ill afford such lavish gifts."

"It wasn't a gift." She pressed her lips together and downed her head, convincing him of her guilt but not her remorse.

"Then what was it, Miss Cardone? Payment for services rendered?"

Her head snapped up and her eyes sparked with indignation and some other emotion he couldn't quite put his finger on. "How dare you think that I— That Cesare and I were more than friends."

"Do not lie to me, Miss Cardone."

"I'm telling you the truth. Cesare is a dear friend and my employer. Nothing more."

He pressed his palms on the desk when he longed to grasp her narrow shoulders and shake the truth from her. "Where the hell did the money go? You certainly haven't spent it on designer clothes or a fancy apartment."

"How would you know?"

"I've seen the small flat you live in and rent." He snorted. "You don't even own a car. Look at me!" he commanded when she looked away. "I want the truth. Why was my father giving you thousands of euros every month on top of your salary?"

She trembled the slightest bit, like a hare cornered by the wolf. "It was a loan."

"A loan," he repeated, and she bobbed her head.

It was a lie. He was sure of it. But he didn't hold any hope that she'd divulge her secrets. Not yet anyway.

"What are the terms of your loan?" he asked, forcing a lighter tone with her now.

She blinked and her soft mouth parted slightly. Could it be she hadn't thought that for every loan there was an agreement of repayment?

She shifted uneasily on the chair and looked everywhere but at him. "It was interest free for the first nine months, so I've not actually made a payment. Cesare agreed that I could wait until the inn was making a modest profit."

This time it was his turn to frown, for his hasty investigation of her revealed she was the daughter of a fisherman from Cinque Terre. Her only family was a grandmother who lived in Manarolo, and a brother who had a weakness for gambling.

He'd been unaware that she owned property, but the fact it was a business raised his suspicions.

"What inn?" he asked, careful to keep his tone casual.

"My family's inn in Manarolo." Her eyes blazed with such passion that his own anger cooled for a heartbeat. "It has been in my family for generations, passing from mother to daughter. Since my mamma died long ago, my nonna and I own it. But it was falling into disrepair. I've refurbished much of it with the money Cesare loaned me. It is beginning to do quite well with tourists."

As well it should, since she'd likely poured a small fortune into the restoration of it. Money that was drained from his father's business!

"Your nine months are up," he said. "Where is your contract so I may review the loan details?"

"Cesare and I had a verbal agreement. He never got around to deciding on a monthly cost I could afford."

"Then I must remedy that for my father," he said, and had the satisfaction of seeing a damning flush steal over her pale cheeks. "I'll have Umberto draw up the papers. Can we agree on payment in full within three months with the first install-ment due the first of the month?"

Her lush lips thinned and he saw a second's uncertainty flicker in her eyes. "Yes, of course."

She agreed far too quickly. More than likely she'd been salting the excess money away. Possibly she'd invested it and could pay back the loan in due time.

But there was the possibility she thought to disappear and then he'd be cheated of his vengeance.

He couldn't let that happen. He had to hold her to their agreement and he knew of only one thing she seemed to prize above everything.

"For collateral, I'll hold your half of the inn until the loan is repaid in full," he said.

"No!" The worry lines deepening on her brow proved she didn't like that idea at all.

"Do you have something else you can put up in its place? Something of similar value?"

"No, nothing," she said.

"Then we have a deal?"

"Yes," she said, though it was more a hiss.

Though Stefano Marinetti prided himself on being a passionate lover, he excelled at coming out on top in any business transaction he entered into.

This was cold, hard business.

Still, his fingers curled around hers, gauging the strength of the delicate bones and admiring the texture of her silken skin. If he was a brutal man, he could crush her hand as surely as he intended to crush her future with Marinetti.

He lifted her hand to his mouth and dropped a kiss on the back of her smooth, small hand. Her gasp echoed in the stillness and vibrated over his skin in a featherlight caress. He felt her telltale tremble before she jerked her hand away, seeming as shaken by her reaction as he was.

"You surprise me, Miss Cardone. I expected a more—" he paused to let his gaze touch the tense curve of her mouth, the too rapid rise and fall of her breasts, then back to her tempting mouth again "—*personal* deal from you."

"What could be more personal than me placing my family's inn up as a guarantee on my loan?"

He sent her a heated smile that deepened her blush. "You. But it is just as well you didn't make such an offer for I would have refused your favors." In fact he'd looked forward to doing just that so she'd know he couldn't be beguiled. So she'd know he was in charge here—in business and in seduction!

Her expressive eyes flared with the fire of anger. "You're vile."

He smiled, for he'd been called far worse. "I simply play to win in all things. Should you fail to make your first payment, I will seize your family's inn."

Then she'd regret the day she set out to deceive his father. Then he'd have the satisfaction of hurting her like she'd hurt his mother.

"You shall have the first payment before the month is out," she said.

"I should hope so, *bella*, since this is the first of the month," he said, and saw genuine shock register in her eyes. "Today is the due date for your first payment."

"No! It can't be."

"I assure you it is. You have until midnight tonight to meet the terms of the loan or forfeit your collateral. Do not bother to ask for an extension or alteration to the terms for the answer will be no. Remember that, Miss Cardone."

CHAPTER THREE

THERE was little chance she'd ever forget that Mr. Arrogant was in total charge of his father's company. And her?

Only temporarily.

"That's less than twelve hours away," she said, fighting the panic that left her trembling inside.

He gave another lazy shrug. "You've owed a first payment for months. Are you conceding defeat?"

"Not at all. I'll have the money by tonight."

Gemma just wished she felt half as sure as she let on.

She had a little money put back and hoped her brother could loan her the rest. It shouldn't be a problem as he'd told her countless times of late that he'd had excellent luck at sea with his fishing business.

But even after that deadline was met, another one loomed in thirty days. And another after that. What a nightmare she'd entered into!

She couldn't continue borrowing money from her family. No, her only recourse would be to take out a loan at the bank. At least then she could get more favorable terms. At least then she wouldn't be subjected to Stefano Marinetti's lurid suggestions.

There was no time like the present to appeal to Cesare's

banker, either. Being indebted to Stefano was simply too stressful for her. Being in the same room with him was nearly more than she could bear.

Since Signora Marinetti's funeral when she'd first seen Stefano across the crowded room, she'd had trouble tearing her gaze away from the man whose bearing commanded her full attention. She'd known he'd bring trouble and change.

She just hadn't dreamed it would touch her so personally. She hated the power he exerted over her as much as she hated the untenable position she was in.

"Your ability to meet the deadline deserves celebration," he said, his voice a rich blend of arrogance and sensuality that whispered over her senses like silk on skin.

"That isn't necessary." Or wanted.

The less she was in his company the better.

He lounged back in his chair and stroked his lower lip with one long, blunt finger, the gesture masculinely contemplative and sexy as hell. "I insist."

"Fine," she said when this arrangement was anything but. "Is there anything else you need?" she asked in her most bland business tone, a contradiction to the riot of emotions going on inside her.

"No, *bella*, that is all," he said.

She stiffened at the endearment, for it was just a phrase to him. Just a toss of words that meant nothing. He likely used it to charm women all the time.

And Stefano Marinetti certainly knew how to flirt!

She marched across the room on legs that trembled, refusing to give in to the urge to run from the man. He'd enjoy seeing her distress, her fear. She'd deny him both.

It was imperative that she maintain her dignity and go about her duties as if nothing out of the ordinary had happened. As if her entire future didn't depend on her meeting this damnable deadline at midnight.

"One more thing," Stefano said the second she'd reached the door and freedom, the velvet timbre in his voice ensnaring her as tightly as a mariner's net. "Make dinner reservations for us at Gervasio."

"I already have dinner plans."

"Cancel them," he said in an obnoxiously imperial tone.

Everything was happening too fast as it was and quickly spiraling out of her control.

She wasted no time leaving the confines of his office where every breath she drew brought the taste of him to her tongue and the clean, spicy scent of him filled her head. The fact that he expected she would prostitute herself infuriated her. But then he believed she was more than his father's personal secretary.

And she could only defend herself so far without revealing Cesare's secret. Dear God, could this get any worse?

Her gaze flicked to the clock and her insides knotted. It wasn't even close to noon and she already felt as if she'd put in a full day's work. She'd be a jumble of nerves well before the deadline tonight.

She took a steadying breath and let it out slowly. Dinner with Stefano at Gervasio. At one time she'd have looked forward to dining in the elite restaurant. But now it loomed as the place where she stood to lose everything, including her pride.

But what choice did she have but to go through with this mad plan?

The money that Cesare withdrew every month was for Rachel's care. But she couldn't tell Stefano that. She couldn't trust him to do what was right for the little girl.

So she'd blurted out that the money was a loan for the inn. *Her* inn. And now he'd set his eye on her half of that!

If only she could tell him the truth. But Stefano had abandoned his family before in their time of need. He seemed to possess no concept of family. He didn't seem to care for anything but money and power.

Now he was taking charge of his father's company and would certainly change Marinetti forever. Her heart ached for Cesare for he'd lost his wife, his health and now control of his own company.

In regards to Rachel, Cesare didn't have any other family he could trust with her care. Nobody but her.

Their bond was so strong. So unshakable. She'd do anything for Cesare. Anything for Rachel. Anything.

Which is why she'd agreed to Stefano's terms. If Cesare didn't trust his son to ensure Rachel continued to receive the best care, then neither could she. *Take care of Rachel until I am able to do so again*, Cesare had told her.

But when would Cesare return? How could she possibly satisfy that staggering loan every month? And the bigger question, how would Cesare continue to care for Rachel if he was indeed close to bankruptcy?

He couldn't, which meant that, too, passed to her.

With a curse, she crossed to her desk and phoned her brother. Since her association with Cesare and her move to Viareggio, she'd rarely seen Emilio.

Though they'd spoken on the phone, even that was difficult to arrange for her brother was at sea for long stretches of time, often out of range of his mobile. That must be the case now for the phone rang and rang.

She hung up and thought it ironic that she was contacting him to beg for a loan. How the tables had turned!

Two years ago it was her brother who was constantly

asking her for money. Neither she nor her papa had realized then that Emilio had adopted the Machiavellian lifestyle.

His reckless gambling had caused their papa untold grief for years. But after the last bout of rehabilitation, her brother had finally settled down and married.

After their father's death, Emilio had taken great interest in the shipping business he'd inherited. His wife helped Nonna with the reopening of the inn and day-to-day management.

Why, her brother had boasted that the money she'd sent home to refurbish the inn had made a tremendous difference in their lives. She could hardly wait to see the changes made to the old inn, but her obligations to Cesare had prevented her from visiting all these months.

Now because of her promise to Cesare, she could lose half of the inn she'd struggled to save. Without pausing to consider the ramifications, she phoned Cesare's banker.

As expected, the man was more interested in Cesare's health than her business, but she managed to gain his promise that he'd assess the market value of the refurbished inn and get back to her on the particulars of a long-term loan. It was a good start, and she'd have thirty days to finalize the details.

Just thinking of the sum left her light-headed. She cradled her head in her hands and fought off a wave of stress-induced nausea. She'd never get out of debt!

But bringing Rachel's image to mind was all it took to convince her she was doing the right thing. Never mind it was the only thing she could do and keep her word.

The intercom came to life and she swallowed a startled squawk.

This wasn't the short zing that Cesare often used to alert her. No, the intercom made a continual buzz like a swarm of angry bees, a sound made possible only if a finger was held on the button to make a noise she couldn't ignore. And God knew she wanted to ignore Stefano at this moment.

"Yes," she answered when the buzzing finally stopped and she could respond.

"I will be meeting with the yard supervisors, managers and assistants throughout the day," Stefano said. "Alert me when the first employee arrives."

"Of course," she said, relieved to know she'd be spared his company.

"I have ordered appetizers for the meeting," he said. "Send the caterer in the minute he arrives."

"I will," she said with gritted teeth, and moments later she did just that.

The caterer had no more than left when the production supervisor strode in. Treating the workers to appetizers was a generous touch and she didn't want to think of Stefano as generous, not when he was being anything but with her.

Gemma shoved thoughts of Stefano's smile and imposing demeanor and heated gazes from her mind. The man had commanded far too much of her time. And wasn't that an ingenious ploy of the playboy billionaire to keep her off balance?

She grabbed the chance alone to ring her brother again. But like before, Emilio didn't answer then or any of the times she tried during the next four hours while Marinetti managers and assistants took their individual meetings with Stefano.

Frustration nipped along her nerves as she tried to contact her brother one last time. If she couldn't reach him and secure the money for that first installment, she'd lose the inn!

Just when she feared all was lost, Emilio answered with his typically effervescent, "*Ciao!*"

Relief that she'd finally caught him left her trembling and

she got a two-handed grip on the phone. "I've been trying all afternoon to reach you. Were you out to sea?"

A long pause pulsed over the line. "*Sì*, I was out. Is something wrong?"

She nearly laughed, for the list was too long to go into, even if she was so inclined. Less was more, she told herself.

"How has business been?"

Emilio cursed, but it was the vehemence in his voice more than the words that gave her new cause for worry. "I have had bad luck. You know how it is."

She did know, for there had been times when their papa had barely managed to put food on their table due to a poor day's catch. It had been worse after their mamma died and their papa had seemed so alone and adrift.

"Yes, I haven't forgotten," she said, and screwed up her courage to do the thing she'd never done. "Emilio, I have a loan that is due and I can't pay it. I need your help in this, and I will repay you in full in a month. Maybe less."

And she would somehow, even though she'd supported her brother and his wife while he struggled to pick up the reins of their father's fishing business. She'd never asked for recompense. Never. Surely her brother would help her now.

"When is your loan due?" he asked.

"Tonight," she said. "Can you manage it?"

Again, another long, uncomfortable pause that did nothing to ease Gemma's doubts.

"*Sì*. I'll bring you the cash, but it may be late," Emilio said. "Okay?"

"Yes, fine. The deadline is midnight." She bit her lip, debating where to meet her brother for the exchange. There was really only one option. "I'm dining with Stefano at Gervasio at ten. If you can't make it by eleven, please call."

"I'll meet you there around that time," he said just as bells sounded in the background—bells that she associated with casino jackpots going off.

"Emilio, are you gambling again?" she asked, gripping the phone like a lifeline, but he'd already hung up.

Worry seeped into her bones like a cold mist rolling in off a winter sea. Were those casino bells? Had her brother reverted to the vice that had nearly destroyed him before?

No, she must be mistaken. He'd been fishing. Perhaps what she'd heard were the chime of bells on nearby ships. Yes, that had to be it.

All would be well. Emilio would lend her the money for the first loan, and she'd secure the rest from the banker. Perhaps once Cesare recovered from surgery he could lift this burden from her. And if he didn't recover?

A chill swept through her blood and left her trembling. She had promised Cesare that she'd hold his secret and she would. She'd promised she'd take care of his daughter while he was unable to. But she hadn't thought she'd have to come up with the money that Cesare had used for his daughter's care each month!

It was a staggering sum, simply because Cesare insisted on the finest for Rachel. And Gemma couldn't deny her, either. The child had been through so much pain in her short life.

If only Stefano put family first like his father did. But he'd been in charge less than a day and had already changed many things. She'd heard the department heads grumbling to themselves as they left his office.

No, she had no choice but to shoulder this alone.

"Did you take lunch?" Stefano asked.

She nearly jumped out of her skin to discover he stood right behind her. Realizing he was that close had her whole system going haywire again.

"No," she said, tidying her already neat desk to keep her hands busy. "The time got away from me."

He said nothing for the longest time, just stood behind her chair. She was intimately aware of each breath he took. Of the spicy scent that was subtle yet powerful all the same.

"Come and take a letter," he said, laying a hand on the back of her chair and just barely grazing her spine with his thumb.

That's all it took for a bolt of energy to hum through her and send her senses reeling again. She lurched to her feet and out of his reach, not caring if her aversion to him was obvious.

His hot gaze snared her for a moment and she flushed at the amusement dancing in those dark, fathomless eyes. My God, nothing got past this man. Nothing!

She grabbed her notepad and marched into his office, eager to take her dictation or notes and get the hell out of here when she was keenly aware of him as a man. And how could she be anything but?

He'd removed his jacket at some point and rolled up the sleeves on his crisp white shirt. She didn't want to notice that his forearms were muscled and generously sprinkled with black hair. She certainly didn't wish to appreciate the male power and beauty of his physique, but it was impossible not to.

She damned her gaze for returning to—no, for lingering on—the wedge of hair visible at the open V of his shirt. Was his chest hair soft? The muscles firm? The deep olive skin hot and smooth?

Again, she was reminded of the hard-muscled gods. Stefano could certainly have been a noble model. And when he chose to turn on the charm, he simply took her breath away.

How in the world was she going to work with this man when being close to him turned her into a weak-kneed ninny?

She couldn't. But she couldn't afford to quit her job and search for another, either, not when she'd have a sizable debt hanging over her.

It was an untenable situation.

He was masculinely beautiful. Sexy as hell. But he was also domineering. Arrogant. And a man she dared not trust with Cesare's deepest secret.

She hurried toward the desk only to find it laden with files. Clearly Stefano was going over every asset of Marinetti with a fine-tooth comb.

What had he said to the supervisors, managers and assistants today? She could only guess that those who'd left with smiles on their faces were assured of their position here. The others who'd scurried out with grim faces? She dreaded to imagine what had been said regarding their future with Marinetti.

"My apologies that so little food is left," he said, successfully coming up behind her and trapping her between his desk and the chair.

With the day she'd had coupled with his commanding nearness her stomach was in knots. She couldn't have tolerated the bruschetta, salamis, olives and cheeses anyway.

"That's okay. A few grapes will suffice for now."

She reached for a red grape, but he was quicker. And much, much too close.

Move, her mind screamed. But her legs refused to obey.

Frustrated, she shot him a sharp look and that was her undoing. His gaze captured hers and her mouth went dry at the naked desire blazing in his dark eyes. No man had ever looked at her like this. Ever.

It was decadent. It was shocking. It was oh, so tempting.

Heat radiated off his big body while his spicy scent ribboned around her, as if to bind her to him. Her other senses exploded with sensual awareness and a want so keen she physically ached.

She'd never experienced anything like it. She certainly didn't want to feel it now, toward him of all people.

"Allow me the pleasure, *bella.*"

"No, really, I'm not—"

He brushed a grape over her lips, slowly, sensuously. Her protest withered in her throat.

Her body tingled and pulsed with a need so powerful she feared her legs would fail her. She wanted to reach for him. To lean on him. To fall into the promise in his darkly mesmerising eyes and forget the world.

Part of her mind that wasn't numbed by lust warned her that she was treading on dangerous ground. Yet she parted her lips and took the ripe fruit from his fingers anyway, unable not to do so.

"Succulent, hmm?" he asked, his thumb grazing her lower lip again and again, then sliding to her chin as his eyes danced with wicked lust and amusement.

She managed a weak nod as sizzling sensations exploded in her mouth and a pulsing need expanded between her legs.

This was a side of Stefano she hadn't seen before, and he was even more devastating to her senses. Never mind that he was arrogantly sure of his sexuality and masculinity. Never mind that he was in a position to call all the shots. Never mind he was taking over Marinetti…and her.

"You must try more of the *insalata di frutta,*" he said, lifting a slice of strawberry to her mouth.

Protesting was out of the question, even if she had a thought to refuse. She took it, thinking to make short work of it. But as the sweet nectar of the fruit slid down her throat, the heat of his thumb brushed her lower lip again.

A fire exploded in her, foreign and thrilling.

She tried to tamp down her desire. Truly she did. But when he sucked the juice off his fingers while his hot gaze dueled with hers, she was lost.

This was passion. Raw and earthy.

She clutched her steno pad to her breast, heart hammering so hard she was certain that he could hear it. "You wanted me to take a letter?"

"I have changed my mind." His eyes took on a dark opaque glint that tossed her nervous reflection back at her.

He rolled a shoulder in a careless shrug and checked his watch. "The workday is nearly over."

A fact she'd looked forward to all day. Yes, she could escape Stefano's dominating presence for a while. But it was a short reprieve, for she was expected to dine with him tonight.

"Is there anything you need me to do before I leave?" she asked, a question she'd posed to Cesare countless times.

"Leave? But our work is far from finished."

"But you said the day was nearly over."

"Here." His smile was positively rapacious. "As I mentioned before, you'll be taking over the role of my secretary as well. You'll join me when I divide my time between Marinetti Shipyard and Canto Di Mare."

Gemma bit her lip, wanting to refuse. But how could she?

Stefano's secretary was away, and Cesare would not be needing her. Combining the positions made sense.

But it denied her a reprieve from Stefano. It forced her to remain in his company for longer hours and suffer this unsettling attraction that arced between them.

"How much later will we work?" she said, letting her annoyance sound in her voice.

"Two, three hours at the most." He shrugged into his suit

jacket and gave each sleeve a sharp tug in turn. "Is there a problem?"

A problem? There were too many for her to count.

She glanced down at the simple skirt and blouse she'd worn to work. "I will need to return home so I can change into suitable clothes for dinner."

Deep lines streaked across his brow. "There won't be time."

"You expect me to wear this?"

Instead of answering, he gave her a long, slow appraisal that scanned her from head to toe. His expression was a combination of indignation and desire that she didn't understand and certainly didn't want. Not from him!

He checked his watch in that impatient way of his. "It is time for us to be off to Livorno."

She didn't bother to hide her annoyance as she retrieved her purse. Was this how it felt to be at his beck and call? To let him choose where you dined? What you wore?

Her gaze fell on her portfolio tucked beneath her desk. That tight, tingling sensation pulled at her stomach. She couldn't go off and leave Cesare's secret files there.

She didn't dare take her bag with her now, not when she was going to be gone half the night with Stefano. Quickly she stuffed it in the back of her file cabinet and locked the door. Nobody had the key but her.

Cesare's secrets and her own would be perfectly safe in there tonight. Tomorrow she'd remove it to her flat.

Tomorrow she'd start off on better footing with Stefano. Tomorrow, he'd have no hold over her.

CHAPTER FOUR

STEFANO guided Gemma to his Alfa Romeo, the sleek silver contours of the 8C *Competizione* glistening like a diamond in the setting sun. But the luxurious car paled in comparison to the flaxen-haired beauty on his arm.

He suspected the tension he felt eddying off her petite form came from her aversion at being forced to remain in his company. Guilt. It had to be guilt on her part, for he was a generous man who had simply stepped in to manage his father's business.

Women loved him. He loved women.

But he detested manipulative *primadonne*.

Gemma Cardone definitely fit that description indeed. She'd charmed Cesare Marinetti into her bed and took him for thousands.

So far she hadn't attempted to get in Stefano's good graces. In fact, she'd seemed horrified over assuming the role of his secretary. Had he been right and she'd thought to flee instead of repaying her "loan"?

How easily lies spilled from her pretty mouth. There'd been no loan, yet she'd said there was instead of admitting the truth of being his father's mistress.

Perhaps she realized that he wouldn't be an easy mark like

Cesare Marinetti. Or maybe she was wily enough to avoid an overture because she knew he'd not accept his father's leavings.

Then again perhaps neither of those reasons applied.

In hindsight, Stefano had stormed into Marinetti Shipping with one thing on his mind—retaliation. Instead of portraying himself in his typical charming manner, he'd been brusque and demanding. What woman would want to warm the bed of such a tyrant?

His only excuse was that his heart was still heavy over his mamma's passing while his blood roared with the need for vengeance. Why had his father's heart failed when he had been driving with his wife? Why hadn't that attack occurred on one of those trips to Milan?

Why had his mamma died instead of this scheming mistress?

There was no answer. He knew that. *Quel che è stato è stato.*

It was his duty to protect his father against Gemma's schemes and honor what was his mamma's last wish. Get rid of Gemma Cardone!

That was the only interest he had with his father's mistress. He did not wish to gain her favor. So why had she wormed her way into his thoughts for most of this day with her big sad eyes and wary smile? Why was she commanding his attention now? Why did his body leap whenever she was near?

Maledizione! He didn't give a damn what Gemma thought about him. She'd gotten all she could for herself.

Now he'd see she paid back a portion of the debt. Once his revenge was sated, he'd fire her. She'd be nothing then but an unpleasant memory.

Sì, it was up to Stefano to rebuild the empire his father had once loved and allow him to heal and cope with his grief. He'd systematically collect what was due Marinetti Shipyard and ensure that Gemma Cardone never approached a Marinetti again.

Pride and honor. He understood both well. He lived by that silent code.

Yet when Gemma slid onto the supple leather seat and gave him a teasing glimpse of long, creamy thighs, his body jerked with a sudden bolt of lust. And why wouldn't he find her attractive?

He was a hot-blooded Italian male and she was a provocative woman. He loved and respected women. He loved to make love to them. He ached to make love with this one!

Though he could neither respect nor like Gemma for the heartache she'd brought his family, she did appeal to him on a purely physical level.

Okay, maybe it was more than that. He was moderately impressed that she had carried on an affair with his father for nine months and managed to cloak their assignations under the guise of business trips. Her cunning was ample reason why he must end this nasty business with her as soon as possible.

He'd stepped in to save Marinetti Shipyard from his father's lapse of good judgment and a calculating woman's machinations. He would not fall victim to her charms, too.

Stefano shut the car door a bit harder than he had intended and swore as the sound echoed his annoyance in the near-empty parking lot. But she barely flinched.

His anger mounted as he rounded the sleek front of his car and threw himself behind the wheel, barely sparing her a glance. She raised an eyebrow, as if chastising him for his show of temper.

And that made his blood boil.

For a woman who stood to lose her historic inn, she seemed suspiciously calm. She must have arranged for the first payment to be met.

Fine! He would take her money tonight. He'd let her win this round, but that would be her last victory.

Annoyance thrummed his nerves as he turned over the powerful engine and steered the car into traffic. The pleasure he usually gained behind the wheel of the luxury automobile was absent.

Gemma occupied his thoughts. He was certain she'd been the reason his parents had launched into a vicious argument—an argument that ended with his father suffering a heart attack and losing control of his car on that fateful night.

He would do well to remember that.

He tightened his fingers on the supple leather steering and for a brief moment wondered if he'd made a colossal error in judgment. When he confronted her about the money she'd taken from his father—the "loan" as she called it—he'd expected her to beg for lenience. He'd thought she'd proposition him into forgiving the debt, or at the least take it out in trade.

He'd never dreamed she'd agree to repay the loan, or that she'd actually come forth with any money. If she did honor that agreement, it would take years for her to repay the debt. He'd never be free of her conniving ways!

And where was the taste of vengeance in that? There would be none.

No, he would not let her off easy. He had to hurt her as she'd hurt his family. The inn seemed to be the key.

The inn that she'd elaborately redesigned with his papa's money!

But even that wasn't enough.

No, he wanted to publicly humiliate her. He wanted all to see her for what she was—a scheming wanton.

Then maybe he'd feel vindicated. Then his mamma's honor would be appeased.

Yes, he'd retain her as his secretary, even if it meant generously extending his own secretary's vacation. From there it should be a simple thing to give the impression that Gemma was much more than an employee.

All he had to do was be less circumspect in his dealings with Gemma and more attentive to her. He had to tamp down his anger and openly flirt with her.

The gossips would do the rest, creating a romance and thereby diverting attention away from his parents' scandal. If she began to believe she was charming him, then all the better.

Watching her hopes rise and then plummet would be a far more satisfying revenge.

"A friend of mine owns a boutique in Pisa," he said as he sped down the coastal *autostrada*. "I am sure you will find a cocktail dress there."

"I see no reason to buy something new when I have perfectly suitable clothes in my flat," she said, her chin lifted in challenge.

Designer clothes that his papa had purchased, or more of the same demure garments like she wore now? Since nobody claimed to have seen his papa and her out on the town, he suspected she hadn't been treated that lavishly.

And of course since she shunned the trappings of a mistress, the liaison had continued with nobody the wiser. Sly. Very sly.

"Consider the dress a gift for your dedication to my father and Marinetti Shipping," he said, forcing a warm smile that he didn't feel.

She didn't voice a protest, but the pinched look on her face said she didn't like this at all.

Stefano's smile deepened. When he was through with her, everyone would know she was his paid paramour.

* * *

Gemma stared at herself in the dressing room mirror, trying without success to block Stefano's rich laugh as he chatted with the designer and flirted with any female who ventured near. She'd looked out earlier to find him lounging in a chair with a glass of wine dangling from his long tanned fingers.

Every move he made was fluid, like a maestro conducting an orchestra. The silent music was a sensual caress that left her skin tingling. Left her restive yet compelled her to sway to the rhythm pounding in her blood.

His aura was so powerful to her senses that she had to literally tear her gaze from him to break the spell.

Mio Dio! How could she find such a callous man attractive?

It vexed her that Stefano had given everyone here the impression they were an item. Protesting would have only drawn more attention to her and the arrogant billionaire, so she closeted herself in the dressing room to try on the selection of dresses that Stefano had chosen.

He'd laughed and said it wasn't necessary to test the fit. And he had been annoyingly right!

The teal cocktail dress fit her to perfection. The color emphasized the blue-green of her eyes and complemented her fair complexion that she'd inherited from her English mother.

The plunging neckline gave more than a teasing peek of the deep valley between her bosom. It also exposed the dainty necklace that her papa had given her.

A sad smile tugged at her mouth as she ran a finger over the pendant suspended on a fine gold chain. How long had he saved to buy the aquamarine surrounded by tiny diamonds? Months? Perhaps a year?

Her fingers tightened around the necklace. It looked insignificant paired with this dress that cost more than two months' wages. But then Stefano's friend was Vanni—a new yet much desired designer!

"Ah, I see you do have jewelry," Stefano said from the doorway of her dressing room, startling her by his boldness. "I hadn't noticed earlier."

"How dare you barge in here!"

His sculpted lips curved into a devilish smile. "You will find I dare many things."

She dreaded to imagine what else he had in store for her.

"The dress fits you to perfection," he said.

She refused to warm to the compliment. "I don't wear daring necklines."

"You should," he said. "It is a shame to cover such beauty."

"Such flattery," she said, trying to sound glib though she trembled inside with anger and that damning sensual pull. "I'm sure you flirt outrageously with every woman you meet."

"*Sì*, but I only compliment the ones who justly deserve it."

She couldn't think of a thing to say to that remark so she just affected a calm she didn't feel and smiled up at him. Meeting his gaze head-on was a mistake.

His dark eyes glittered with amusement and passion, and the firm line of his mouth curved into a disarming smile, transforming him from the hard resolute man into a devilish charmer. Her knees went weak and her insides trembled in an erotic hum of desire.

He reached out and stroked a finger down her cheek, and the control she'd fought to maintain shattered into a billion shards of new sensations. "You are beautiful, *mio caro*."

She reached behind her and grasped the dressing room curtain to steady herself when every fiber in her body ached to reach out to him. What was happening to her?

Yes, he was devastatingly attractive, but she hated what he

stood for. She hated the power he wielded over her. She hated him for storming into her peaceful, quiet life and turning it into a maelstrom of emotions in just one day.

"Thank you, but I'd like to try on something else." Something less revealing. Something that wouldn't make her feel sophisticated and desirable.

"There is no time. Come."

She bit her lip, torn between protesting or going meekly along as a lamb to the slaughter. "I refuse to leave here in this dress."

"Very well, but make it a short moment." He backed from the dressing room, but the spice of his cologne remained to tease her senses.

Gemma drew in a shaky breath and then another, angry and aroused and confused in turn. She felt vulnerable. Alone.

Silly emotions to feel since they'd be surrounded by other people in the restaurant. It wouldn't be long and her brother would join them and she'd meet Stefano's first payment.

And if Emilio didn't show up?

She refused to think that as she donned her sensible clothes and left the dressing room with the new dress hanging on the hook.

Stefano was waiting for her, but instead of hurrying her out the door, he waited until the assistant hurried forward with his purchase carefully covered in an opaque garment bag.

She certainly didn't want him buying anything for her. This dress far exceeded any bonus she'd earned from her job and was far too revealing to wear to work. And what was he thinking anyway by buying her clothes when she was already indebted to him?

"You should have foregone this bit of shopping," she said as Stefano escorted her to the sleek silver car that had attracted a small crowd. "The delay will make you late for your business meeting."

"It's nothing that can't be made up in driving time," he said as he helped her into the butter-soft leather passenger seat and then quickly slid behind the wheel.

The thought of racing to their destination sent alarm zinging along her nerves. But as the car sped along the highway, she found herself enjoying the view of the islands strung into the Ligurian Sea like emeralds floating on the foam-edged blue waters.

She supposed to any passerby they looked like a couple out enjoying the evening. But that was just an illusion.

There was nothing casual about her being with Stefano tonight. This was pure business. The question was where would the night end? With her free of his hold, or more firmly caught in his grasp?

She instinctively lifted a hand to her neck, a gesture that had become habit when she was anxious. But toying with the necklace would only draw attention to her nervousness and Stefano would surely use that to his advantage.

Her hand fluttered back to her lap. "Did you say your company offices are in Livorno?"

"The offices and the shipyard," he said. "The hull on Canto Di Mare's new thirty-five meter yacht is finished and waiting for my approval."

"Another hulking superyacht to crowd the Mediterranean?"

He laughed, a rich baritone that had the power to soothe her tense nerves. "I see you have adopted my father's view on big pleasure ships."

"We held much the same beliefs," she admitted.

"Such as?"

"More of the wealthy should put their money to better use

than on sating their own selfish pleasures." She glanced his way and noted the tightening of his artfully sculpted lips and narrowing of his mesmerizing eyes. "Or on the proliferation of unnecessary diversions."

Despite the warm breeze riffling her hair and caressing her skin, she felt the chill as he closed off from her. She'd clearly struck a raw nerve by bringing up money.

"Not all *miliadario* have a philanthropic heart."

"More is the pity." When she thought of how much good just a portion of that extravagance would do, she grew angry.

"I suppose you discussed this issue with my father?" he asked, the bite in his tone hinting his anger was rising as well.

"I didn't have to," she said.

"Meaning?"

"Your father is a generous, caring man," she said instead, and that truth seemed to make him all the more angry.

Gemma turned her attention to the harbor and managed to draw air into her lungs. Very few fishing boats could be seen amid the staggering array of yachts and trawlers.

The old way of life was nearly gone, and with it she feared a good deal of those compassionate values were disappearing as well. The same could be said for the good men like her father and Cesare, too.

She had felt comfortable with Cesare from the start. He had been the friend she could talk with about her deepest fears. He listened. He applauded her bravery and her compassion.

She loved him. Respected him. She'd do all she could to protect him.

But who would protect her from Stefano Marinetti and his smoldering sensuality?

Stefano pulled his car into a slot and tossed her a teasing look that was at odds with his earlier pique. His rapier fire switch in emotions kept her on edge. That was likely just what he wanted to do.

After all, she was a very small fish in a big sea and he was the whale who could swallow her whole.

"We have much to do in a short period of time," he said as he unfolded his long, lean form from the car then collected the bags the designer had given him.

He must expect her to change clothes here. What she wouldn't give for a shower!

"I assume you have a list you wish me to attend to," she said as she quit the car, not about to wait for him to open her door.

The deep crease between his eyes hinted he disliked her independence. "Most of the daily duties have been seen to by my staff here. All that is left for you to do is retrieve messages and see to the necessary correspondence."

Typical secretarial duties that anyone could have seen to during the day, including a temp. It hadn't been necessary for him to drag her along. No, there was another reason why he'd monopolized her time. She feared it had something to do with Cesare and her part in his life.

If he'd only spent time with his dear father these past years he wouldn't be left in the dark now! But he'd made his decision to leave the family business and the division cost Cesare untold grief for he'd lost not just one child but two. One had been the result of an accident. The other had been an intentional separation from the family—a split that was nearly unheard of in Italy.

Here sons and often daughters carried on the family tradition generation after generation. It had been the way for her family, with Emilio taking over their papa's fishing business while she would one day inherit the old inn in Manarolo.

This passing of power was how it should have been with

Stefano Marinetti. When his brother died, he should have assumed that role within the company.

But he'd walked out on his father.

He'd shunned tradition and his *famiglia*.

And what did that say about the man who held his family in so little regard?

He was self-absorbed. Stefano seemed to care for one thing—himself.

Now he was in charge of Marinetti. He'd likely change a company that was steeped in tradition. All to leave his indelible mark.

If not for her promise to Cesare, she'd leave now. But she was honor bound to stay. She couldn't trust Stefano with Rachel's care, not for a moment.

With her gown slung over one broad shoulder, he guided her into the new building that was open and spacious. Of course it would look larger since it was past hours and the employees had gone home for the day.

She gave the workstations they passed an enviable glance. New computers, new phones and ergonomic chairs that screamed comfort. But then Stefano had the money to splurge on such niceties.

Cesare had a desperately ill child to provide for. He had obligations to his family. He didn't put money before honor!

Gemma stared out of the expansive stretch of glass windows at the sea and sighed. How different things would be if Stefano was as caring and passionate about life and family as his father was.

She would've found him irresistible. She may actually have given in to the desire that simmered between them, only because she would've found it impossible to say no.

If he was like Cesare, it would be oh so easy to fall in love with him.

But he wasn't like his father.

Stefano was an arrogant aristocrat. No, make that an arrogant, *selfish* aristocrat.

Men like him didn't marry poor working girls like her. They made them their mistresses.

"Is something wrong?" he asked.

She shook her head and bit back a bitter laugh over her errant thoughts. "I am tired. It's been a long day." A long trying day in his company.

"It is far from over." He pushed into an elegantly appointed suite that was clearly his domain and draped the garment bag over a leather sofa. "If you wish to freshen up before you dress, my *bagno privata* is through that door."

She flicked a glance in that direction and nodded before admiring the vista afforded from the windows again. "The view is fabulous."

He shrugged off her observation. "It is never boring."

How typical of the playboy who tired of things far too quickly! She trailed him across the room and through a door, anxious for him to conclude his business here.

For she'd not be able to breathe easy until she'd satisfied that first payment on the awful loan she'd been forced to admit to. Once that was over, she'd be nothing more than his secretary until Cesare returned.

He entered a smaller yet still spacious room where an elegant teak desk sat with an equally gorgeous view of the harbor.

"My personal assistant's office." He pointed to an inbox overflowing with envelopes. "Please sort through these and bring me the ones that need my immediate attention."

She looked at the pile that likely had accumulated for over a week. "Of course."

He glanced at his watch. "I'll be back in thirty minutes."

With that he was off, his long legs carrying his lean, enticing form through the door and out of sight.

Gemma gave the stack of correspondence a glance. It was thrice the size she handled for Cesare every day, but at least the time would pass quickly.

But before she tackled this task, she wanted to shower and be ready to leave when Stefano returned.

She walked the length of his office en route to the *bagno*. Again she was struck with the Spartan elegance surrounding her.

A colorful Laurus Murano vase here. An Alberto Sughi oil there. And the furnishings… They were classic and high quality.

It didn't dawn on her that she and Stefano had similar tastes until she made to flip the lock to ensure privacy. There was none, just a simple catch on the bathroom door.

She hesitated, torn between refreshing herself with a shower and risking being caught in the nude by Stefano.

Gemma bit her lower lip and checked her watch. He wouldn't return for nearly thirty minutes. She'd be done way before then.

Without giving herself time to change her mind, she undressed and stepped into *la doccia* which was certainly large enough for two.

Standing in the shower with warm water pelting her tired body was a refreshing break after a tense day. She did not want to think of Stefano, yet even as warm water pelted her tense muscles she imagined his gaze caressing her. Probing magnetic eyes that could adore and scold in turn.

It annoyed her that thoughts of him invaded her private moments. Couldn't she block him from her mind at all?

She stepped from the shower and wrapped herself in a thick, thirsty towel that swallowed her. These had to have been specially ordered for Stefano's big frame, and just thinking of him stripped to the skin and wet left her trembling with want.

How could she possibly desire a man she didn't respect?

A brisk toweling and she quickly donned her new teal dress. She hated that he'd purchased it, but she loved the design. She'd never owned anything this exquisite.

How could something so simple be so sensual? She didn't know and surely didn't wish to project that aura around Stefano.

She'd repay him for the gown, even though it would take time. She would not be beholden to him.

Gemma quit the bathing room to find Stefano lounging in the doorway. His hot gaze roamed the length of her slowly, pausing at her mouth, her breasts and the juncture of the thighs.

Desire speared low in her belly, more intense than she'd ever felt before. She tightened her hold on the door, knowing she should look away but finding it impossible to tear her gaze from his magnetic stare.

Even the air was charged with an energy that make her skin sizzle and burn as if she'd brushed too close to the sun.

This was lust. Bold. Sensual. Tempting.

Oh, so very tempting.

And dangerous.

Stefano Marinetti was the embodiment of seductive Italian males that one read about, only on a pinnacle above the others. This was the primo playboy who always had a bevy of woman lusting after him.

She'd quickly learned that he'd refined flirting to a fine art. He could adore every inch of the woman he was with and make her feel as if she were the most desired woman in the world. As if she were the *only* woman in the world for him.

He was the kind of man young girls dreamed about, and the one that mammas and papas feared.

He'd take what he wanted from a woman, and toss her aside when he tired of her.

"*Bella*. You take my breath away."

"Thank you," she said, finding it difficult to breathe normally around him. "But I'm sure you're exaggerating."

"Not in the least."

She didn't know what to say to that statement. In true Italian form, he could argue fiercely one moment and revert into the flirt the next.

Now that was an image she didn't wish to conjure up about him. But the idea was in her head and growing stronger, thanks to the sensual energy that crackled in the air, leaving her tingling from head to toe.

"I am a lucky man to have you as my dinner companion tonight," he said.

How could he make a business dinner sound intimate? A business dinner that was a step above blackmail for her? How could he for a moment make her forget the dire importance of this night to her future?

"Shouldn't we be leaving for Viareggio?"

"There is something I must do first, something I have wanted to do since we met."

Stefano pushed away from the doorway and crossed to her with the grace of a jungle cat on the prowl, all sleek muscle and feral energy.

This time there was no doubt he made love to her with his eyes. There was no doubt that she saw her own needs reflected in the smoldering depths of his own.

"What would that be?" she managed to ask, holding her ground because she simply couldn't force her feet to move.

He reached for her, threading the fingers of both hands through her hair to curve over her scalp. The move was as much an anchor as a caress. She knew he meant to kiss her.

Though her mind was screaming at her to run, her body was instinctively bowing into his.

"No," she breathed, a feeble refusal at best, but she found it difficult to do more as his mouth swept down to hers.

Not surprising, he didn't listen to her.

That first crush of his mouth on hers sent new sensations rocketing through her. She swayed, certain she'd have crumbled if he hadn't been holding her close.

Dio mio! He kissed her with a ravenous intensity that thrilled and terrified her, for she knew if he unleashed his sensual appetite on her she'd be powerless to stop him.

More, she'd be powerless to stop herself from surrendering to the promise in his kiss, his touch. In the strong arms that held her fast.

She slammed both hands against Stefano's broad chest to end this madness. But instead of pushing him away as she'd intended, her palms lost their purchase on his silken shirt.

"*Bella*," he breathed, holding her fast and deepening the kiss.

Her splayed fingers pressed against the breadth of his chest. He was so big. So powerful.

Touching him was like touching the sun. Sizzling, erotic heat spiraled through her.

She'd surely burn to a crisp if she stayed too close. But her attempt to push him away was feeble at best. She couldn't think of anything but the intense pleasure engulfing her.

A low groan rumbled from him. He pulled her flush against his body without a break in the kiss that was now singing through her senses with the passion of an aria.

She wasn't a neophyte to kissing, but she'd waited all her

life to have a man make love to her with his mouth like this. This slow dueling of tongues and adoration of lips. Unchained. Earthy. Passionate.

She was awash in a froth of longing with him the center of her universe, the sun that fired her blood. Her arms slipped around him as if to anchor him close now.

Not that she needed to.

One of his hands cradled her head while the other made a long, leisurely caress that was so seductively gentle it brought tears to her eyes. She'd never been touched so emotionally before. It thrilled and terrified her, and like a moth to the flame she kept inching closer for more.

And he gave her more. Not in a bold push as she'd expected but a more languid exploration of her mouth and body—an adoration really.

His lips sipped at the corner of her mouth before he lifted his head. She groaned in protest of the kiss ending too soon and looked up into his eyes.

The glimmer of desire was fading, replaced by a harder glint that smacked of mockery. Suddenly she was all too aware of standing in his embrace, her breasts pressed to his chest, her belly flush with the flat planes of his abdomen, and the hard evidence of his desire pulsing between them.

"I want *fare l'amore* and so you do," he said, gently pushing her from him and gliding a finger down her flushed cheek. "But we must return to Viareggio and our appointed dinner. Later, hmm?"

It took a moment for her dazed brain to register what he was implying. She scrambled out of his reach, hating his cool assumption that she was his for the taking now. Hating herself even more for letting this situation spiral out of control.

"No, not later," she said. "Not ever."

The mouth that had moved with sensuous intent on hers thinned to a hard line. The amorous glint in his eyes died, replaced with a flash of annoyance before narrowing on her.

"We will see," he said.

She shook her head in answer, for it was pointless to argue with him.

He was a playboy, arrogantly sure of his prowess and blessed with a beautiful face and physique of the gods. He was rich and sought after and likely believed every woman he met would gladly crawl into his bed.

She'd been too awed by the sensations he'd wrought to consider he'd take her eagerness to kiss him as a sign that she wanted more. But what did she really know about seduction?

Stefano shrugged into a suit jacket, looking for all the world like a demanding tycoon again. "We must leave now."

"Of course."

She suffered his hand at the small of her back as he guided her out of the building. She certainly didn't want to feel this burning pull toward him, but she couldn't squash it, either.

Yes, the sooner they got this business over with, the sooner she and Stefano could settle into a suitable work arrangement as secretary and boss.

Then she'd count the days until Cesare returned to the helm and Stefano was nothing more than a memory.

CHAPTER FIVE

AN HOUR later, Stefano pulled to the curb of the restaurant and set the brake. He shouldn't have kissed her. He shouldn't have let his hands learn the contour of her breasts, the dip of her waist, the curve of her hips.

He damned sure shouldn't have enjoyed every second she'd been in his arms. But he had, and the only thing that soothed his pride was the fact she'd become as lost in the moment as he.

Now she sat as far from him as possible and stared pensively out the window, quiet and withdrawn, as if bitten by guilt for nearly succumbing to lust. It made the drive back to Viareggio overly long.

But then he was not of a mood to engage in chitchat, either. His own lack of control vexed him. He'd not been the one to stop. She had.

Her body had instinctively reacted to his, pressed to his and moving in a most delicious rhythm of desire. She couldn't deny that!

But she'd come to her senses first. He'd become so intoxicated by a woman's taste and texture that he'd lost focus. He would've taken her right then and there.

Her refusal to engage in an affair with him was a jab to

his ego. For her withdrawal wasn't part of the game of pursuit, the age-old attack and parry ritual of courtship that heightened desire.

This was a firm no.

Something far stronger than lust kept her from succumbing to passion. Loyalty to Cesare Marinetti?

He slid her a glance. Did she believe that when his father recovered they would resume their affair? Did she think because his papa was widowed now that she could assert herself into the role of his wife?

The very idea was galling, for this situation with Gemma smacked of another woman who'd had designs on gaining the lion's share of Marinetti Shipyard.

Before his sister-in-law had got her claws into his brother, she'd been Stefano's lover at university. He'd never thought to introduce her to his family. But that holiday she'd been alone with nowhere to go.

Bringing her home had been the decent thing to do. She had seen it as the opportunity to better her lot in life.

Once she had realized that Stefano's brother was the heir, it had taken her merely a week or two at the most to seduce his brother.

Her deceit had taught him a valuable lesson, for though he hadn't lost his heart to her, he'd certainly lost his head.

But she was far from done with Stefano.

From that point on she'd succeeded in driving a wedge between him and his brother. That had been the major reason he'd left Marinetti Shipyard. He couldn't tolerate being around her and deal with her lies. He wouldn't suffer his brother's distrust of him in business or being around his conniving wife.

His mamma knew the truth, and he suspected his papa did, too, but neither brought it up.

Their new daughter-in-law quickly got with child. The next heir to the shipyard. The first Marinetti grandson which both his parents had doted on.

It had been easier for Stefano to strike out on his own than to cause more strife in his own family. He made his mark and set his own dream for a new shipping company into motion.

But even after the tragic accident that took his brother's, sister-in-law's and nephew's lives he couldn't return to Marinetti. His father still scoffed at his innovations, and refused to compromise.

Yet here he was, thrust into the role of manager. Forced to contend with another scheming woman who had designs on Marinetti Shipyard.

Did Gemma hope to take his mamma's place?

It was a possibility Stefano couldn't ignore for she'd managed to gain a small fortune in a short amount of time. But the stress of keeping up with a young lover and hiding his affair from his wife—no, the world!—had damned near killed his father.

With his mamma dead, there was nothing to stop his papa from easing his grief in Gemma's arms. Nothing but Stefano.

He couldn't tolerate his father making Miss Cardone his wife. He couldn't see his mamma's memory dishonored so. He'd not stand by while another gold-digger bled a Marinetti dry!

He'd turned his back the last time. He wouldn't make that mistake again!

Stefano climbed from behind the wheel and nodded to the waiting attendant. A few lights flashed from the line of trim poplars at the side.

He immediately schooled his features, though any damage

would already be done. He'd caught the attention of the paparazzi who had staked out the restaurant in hopes that a celebrity would happen by tonight. They typically chose an image that conveyed the greatest emotion and slapped some idiotic caption on it.

The media hounds were a nuisance he'd learned to live with. But Gemma and his father had smoothly evaded any limelight on their trysts to Milan.

Of course up until his mamma's untimely death, his parents had been free of the paparazzi for ten years. His insides twisted at the memory.

The deaths of his brother and his family had drawn the gossips in hoards and had driven his parents into hiding.

Stefano remembered well how the journalists had camped out on the edge of their property, waiting for the chance to capture their grief. Vultures, all of them.

Since then Stefano had done all in his power to evade publicity as well. Thankfully time had tempered his animosity.

But this business with Gemma had his old resentment bubbling to the surface again. She was the opposite of his sister-in-law in looks and disposition yet was just as cunning and manipulative.

Gemma had awakened passionately fierce emotions in him that he'd vowed never to fall victim to again! Yet hadn't he done just that when he'd kissed her in his office?

He was not above seducing her to satisfy his lust, but he would not surrender his pride or his head to her.

He wouldn't let history repeat itself!

Stefano rounded the Alpha Romeo with quick angry strides as an attendant helped Gemma get out. More lights flashed from the perimeter and people on the sidewalk stopped to see what celebrity was dining here tonight.

Gemma cast a frantic glance his way and for a moment he almost felt pity for her. Almost.

He offered his arm out of duty and she latched on to it. Though he had zero respect for her duplicity, he was man enough to admit she was a beautiful, desirable woman. Even without the attention of the paparazzi, heads would have turned toward her.

Sì, their pictures would grace the gossip rags tomorrow. Speculation would be ripe of the identity of his dinner companion.

It was just a matter of time before someone recognized her as his father's secretary. Then the gossips would question if this was a business dinner, or something more intimate.

"*Buonasera, Signor Marinetti*!" the host said as Stefano pressed his fingers to Gemma's slender back to guide her to the podium. "Your private room is ready."

"*Grazie*!"

He knew she was a schemer and manipulator, yet his body quickened whenever he touched her. He should be imagining her slaving to repay what she'd stolen instead of picturing her lounging on a bed with her arms reaching for him.

Damning his inability to douse his lust where she was concerned, he hurried her along in the host's wake down an intimately lighted hall. The telling stiffening of her back proved she was eager to break contact with him as well.

Could she be fighting her own desires? Or was she simply playing hard to get so his indomitable male pride would goad him to pursue her?

She could end up married to his father!

No, he wouldn't let that happen.

He'd take her first, make her his paramour and make damn sure the world knew it. That was the only way that his father would see her for what she truly was.

His father was old school. He saw no harm in engaging in an affair, but he'd never tolerate his wife or lover doing the same.

The private dining room held just the right ambiance of subdued light and *serenate violino* drifting in from the main room. It was an area perfectly suited for a lover's tryst.

Or the cutting business he intended to finalize tonight.

He smiled and seated Gemma to his right, confident he was in control of the woman and the situation drawing near.

The waiter bustled in, the lines of his broad face carved in a deep smile. "*Buonasera, signor and signora. Che cosa volete da bere?*"

"Barolo, ten or twelve years old," Stefano said.

"Excellent choice, signor." The waiter smiled at Gemma. "Signora?"

"A *crodino*, please," Gemma said.

She ordered a *bevande analcoliche* at this time of night? "Is there another wine or *apertif* you would prefer?" Stefano asked. "Perhaps a *bellini?*"

She shook her head. "I rarely drink alcohol."

But there were occasions, he was sure. So why not share a celebratory drink with him now?

Perhaps there was another reason why she hesitated to imbibe. Perhaps *vino* loosened her inhibitions. Perhaps she feared she'd lose the tenuous control she'd managed to maintain since they'd left Canto Di Mare.

Perhaps she was remembering the passion that had flared between them when they'd kissed. When his hands had glided over her body. When he'd pulled her close and let her feel the hard evidence of his desire.

Stefano felt the first stirrings of desire in his groin. He usually had far more self-control than that around women, yet with Gemma it seemed nonexistent. Had she had that same effect on his papa?

Likely so. While the old man grew indulgent from his *vino*, she'd kept her wits by drinking an orange fizz. She'd remained in control while his papa slowly lost his!

Just remembering her role in his father's life gouged his anger up another notch. But his anger was equally aimed at himself this time.

If only his mamma had told Stefano of her suspicions months ago perhaps a lot of grief and lost revenue could have been avoided.

He would have spoken with his father.

Yes, they would have argued fiercely, for no man cares to admit he was a fool over a woman—even a hot-blooded Italian who lives to love women. If his father would've realized what Gemma was after, she wouldn't have dipped so deeply into Cesare Marinetti's pockets.

But Stefano had removed himself from his father's business before his brother's death. And afterward? Nothing had changed his father's view of the world. Nothing had opened his eyes to the pollution he was leaving the future generation to clean up.

After Davide's funeral, his father had taken Stefano aside. "Are you ready to give up playing inventor of eccentric ships and return to the family shipyard?"

That fierce Marinetti pride had kept Stefano from asking his papa if he'd needed or wanted his help. Pride and deep involvement launching a new class of eco-friendly seagoing vessels, he amended.

"No," he'd said, and walked out of his papa's life again.

He refused to return to Marinetti Shipyard and be nothing more than a figurehead. He refused to assume his brother's role and be groomed to one day take over the shipyard. He refused to give up his dream now that it was within his grasp.

He'd never been able to see eye to eye with his papa regarding business. Neither of them would bend.

A damned shame it had taken another death for his papa to finally ask for his help. Still nothing had changed.

His father had placed the business in his hands but had insisted that any major changes be discussed with him first. He'd agreed only because he hadn't wished to cause his father undo stress in his condition.

But vengeance simmered in him as he thought of being near the woman who'd come between his father and mamma. He'd known he'd make her pay for all the hell she'd put his mamma through.

That alone was reason enough for Stefano to despise Gemma Cardone. While forcing Gemma to repay every euro she'd conned out of his father was just punishment, it would take years for her to do so even with the plump salary she drew as Cesare's personal secretary.

No, he had to get her out of his father's life for good. The only way to do that was to make her his paramour!

Stefano set his menu aside and studied the little schemer in the mellow candlelight. She looked pale and vulnerable as she stared at the menu, like a waif washed ashore and in need of a protector.

Yes, no wonder his father had fallen under her spell. Now it was time to turn the tables on her.

"They are noted for their calamari," Stefano said in a conversational tone that he used to put adversaries at ease. "But of course feel free to order whatever you wish."

"I couldn't do such a meal justice," she said.

A typical excuse from women who were obsessed with

maintaining a model's figure. All they wanted was a bit of cajoling so they wouldn't feel guilty about indulging!

Not that Gemma had to fret about gaining weight. She was edging toward the painfully thin side already.

"A bit of antipasto will awaken your appetite," he said. "Perhaps *zuppa* as your primo."

"Please, I'm really not hungry."

First her refusal to drink alcohol and now her lost appetite. Was she playing some game to dupe him, or was she beset by an increased case of nerves?

The waiter arrived with his wine and a glass *bicchere* holding her orange fizz. He served the lady first, then he gently poured a dram of wine in Stefano's glass and stepped back to dutifully wait his approval.

Stefano noted the bouquet had a slightly spicy, sweet fragrance much like the one Gemma wore. He frowned, annoyed that comparison came to mind. With effort he concentrated on his opinion of the *vino*.

"Signor?" the waiter asked.

Stefano pushed thoughts of Gemma aside and gave a clipped nod of approval. "*Delizioso.*"

The waiter smiled and proceeded to rattle off the house specials. "What would the lady like?"

"*Un insalata e bruchetta,*" Gemma said.

Stefano tapped the menu on the table. "You must have more than that." Before she could protest, Stefano ordered antipasto and calamari for two. "My mamma always maintained that they serve the best *dolce.*"

She wet her lips and he knew she was tempted. "I shouldn't."

Ah, but she wanted dessert.

He found her willpower annoying and admirable.

"How is Cesare today?" she asked.

She gave the impression she was as delicate as the crystal stem of the glass he clutched in his hand. But he knew there was steel in her spine. Not enough, though.

He could snap the wineglass as easily as he would break her. *Mio Dio*, right now he wanted to do both!

Soon, he told himself. He'd satisfy his revenge soon.

He waited to reply as the waiter bustled in with the platter of antipasto and then left them to their privacy. Those few moments seemed to make her more anxious.

"Papa is stable and resting," he said.

A slight smile touched her mouth, but her expansive sigh relayed her relief and drew his attention to the quick rise and fall of her bosom. "I've been worried."

More likely she was concerned about her future role in his papa's life! He speared shrimp, smoked tuna and vegetables onto his plate and let his anger ebb again. Her cushy lifestyle was crashing to an end around her, whether she realized it or not.

What did she value above all else?

By her own admission she'd invested a lot of money in her family's inn in Manarolo—an inn that she held half ownership in. As he was aware exactly how much money she'd gained from his father, the refurbished inn must rival a five-star hotel on the Riviera!

Still, he found it interesting that she'd put up her shares as collateral on her loan. Even with improvements, he couldn't imagine her assets would come close to covering his father's loss, but if she and her family relied on the income from the inn, he could yank that security blanket out from under her.

"Tell me more about your family's inn on Manarolo."

Genuine excitement lit her eyes and he knew he was on the right track. "It's a wonderful old house nearly five hundred years old. At least half of that time it's been in our family."

"Your mother's family?" he asked as he passed the anti-pasto to her and insisted she eat.

"No, my papa's." She picked a pitiful few items off the platter—no wonder she was skin and bones! "The inn had passed from generation to generation to the oldest girl, but all Nonna had was Papa. So when Mamma gave birth to me, Nonna gave me half of the inn and let Mamma manage it for me. But when she died, it was up to Nonna to see to the inn and care for my brother, Emilio, and me while Papa fished."

It was an arrangement he'd heard of with other working class Italians. Though he was curious about her mother's death at such a young age, he didn't wish to discuss the subject. Perhaps his own mamma's untimely death was still too fresh on his mind.

"Your nonna continues to manage the inn then?" he asked, knowing full well Gemma couldn't have done so the past year because she'd been busy bilking his father out of thousands of euros.

"With my sister-in-law's help."

He popped a succulent shrimp in his mouth and chewed thoughtfully. He could have her past more thoroughly investigated, but that would take time. His patience had nearly run its course.

"What of your brother?" he asked. "Does he and his wife own the other half of the inn?"

"No," she said, the denial swift and firm. "Emilio inherited Papa's fishing business but decided to move it to La Spezia. He said it made good sense to base the business there where he'd be bringing in his day's catch, and he didn't mind taking the train from Manarolo each morning."

Did she honestly believe that?

In the short time he'd had to look into Gemma Cardone's

past, he'd discovered her brother strove to live the life of a playboy. His frequent visits to the Monte Carlo gaming tables were well-known, as was his debatable talent at poker.

The question was where had her brother come by his original bankroll?

Stefano doubted it was from fishing.

He suspected Gemma had fed her brother's gambling habit with the money she'd gained from Cesare in hopes of doubling her family's fortune. But had he been successful?

Rumor had it that Emilio Cardone had been on a losing streak of late. A destructive losing streak. What more had he sold in order to gamble?

"I do worry about Nonna," she said, drawing his attention back to her.

There was genuine concern in her voice. While Stefano was curious what troubled her so, he refused to be moved by it.

"Why? Is your grandmother in poor health?"

She shook her head. "She seems hearty enough, but I know that my sister-in-law lets Nonna do the bulk of the work."

"A bit of a shirker?" Like Cardone?

"She's young and has a baby that demands her time."

Stefano sipped his wine and let it all sink in. Around one year ago life for the Cardones had changed drastically thanks to Gemma becoming Cesare Marinetti's secretary.

"I am curious how you came to work for my father," he said.

She took a bite of mozzarella-topped tomato, stalling to answer he was sure. "I was in Milan attending university and we happened to meet."

Stefano had made his fortune by his ability to read people. Right now he knew Gemma Cardone was lying through her straight pearly teeth. He suspected she was in Milan trolling for an easy victim who would support her and her worthless brother.

"Milan is a big city," he said. "You were lucky to meet my father there, let alone be offered a job that you sought."

"I am well aware of my good fortune," she went on but carefully avoided meeting his eyes.

He stabbed a prosciutto-wrapped mushroom and ate it without appreciating its rich flavor.

To make Gemma suffer for the grief she had put his mamma through, all he had to do was seize control of her inn. That would be easily accomplished if she failed to make that first loan payment by midnight.

He'd own the hotel and Gemma Cardone. He would make her life hell.

The waiter returned with their main course, but Gemma showed little interest in the sumptuous meal. She sipped her orange soda and checked her watch.

The deadline was an hour away, and the calm she'd exhibited earlier was quickly fading. The frown marring her smooth brow hinted that things were not going as she'd planned.

"Is something wrong?" he asked as he refilled his wineglass, determined to remain unmoved by her growing distress.

"My brother was supposed to meet me here."

The vintage wine threatened to sour on his tongue. How dare she invite someone to join them at dinner without consulting him!

"Why?"

Her gaze lifted to his and this time there was no mistaking the worry in their depths. "He is bringing the loan money. Would you mind if I ring him?"

He raised his glass in a mock salute and affected a smile. "Please, do."

So this was her game. She'd claim some emergency had kept her brother from arriving on time so the loan payment would be late. He was sure she'd beg for an extension. And he was sure another minor event would prevent that payment from arriving on time. And so it would go on.

She was about to learn that he was wise to these tactics. That he couldn't be charmed like his father. That he wasn't an easy mark.

This was business.

He excelled at crushing deals.

He wouldn't be moved by tears, hysterics or pleading.

If she failed to honor her part of the contract, he'd take possession of her shares of the inn and her!

"Emilio," she said into her trim mobile phone, an urgency in her voice that lifted the hairs on his nape. Her frown deepened on a pause. "Emilio?"

She looked at Stefano, her smooth brow furrowed in a deep frown. "There must be something wrong with the connection. He answered, but then all I could hear was bells and a crush of voices in the background. Then the call just ended."

Sounds associated with a party. Or more likely the casinos, he thought as he watched her punch in the number again with a finger that clearly trembled.

Hadn't his friend mentioned he'd be testing his luck at a high stakes poker game tonight? It was the same one that Cardone had lost a small fortune at last week.

Time crawled before she ended the call. She looked at him with eyes swimming with concern. Such an accomplished actress!

"Emilio isn't answering." She brushed back her wealth of sun-kissed hair with an impatient hand. "Something must be wrong."

This was a stall tactic on her part and he'd have none of it. It was time she accepted the consequences of her own actions.

"Perhaps your brother is involved in a game."

"Game?" she parroted.

"Poker. He's spent long days in Monte Carlo the past week," he said. "But his luck has deserted him and he's down to bartering his assets to gamble."

She went still, her face leached of color and her eyes far too huge for her gamine face. Prey. She looked like prey, and in that tense moment he was gripped by the urge to protect instead of ruin her.

Maledizione! How could she stir such emotions in him?

"No! He wouldn't do that."

"I assure you he has done exactly that. Two weeks ago I accepted one of his trawlers to bankroll him in a game." An aged gas-guzzling behemoth that caused more pollution than it was worth, but Stefano gladly paid the price just to get it off the waters.

Had he known then about Gemma and her wastrel brother, he'd have stayed in the game that had soon bored him just to bring her brother down. For it was clear that Gemma had made sure that the two of them profited greatly off his papa's largess.

That was just the reminder he needed to harden his resolve. "If I hadn't bought the trawler then someone else would have."

"No! Emilio can't still be gambling," she said, shaking her head. "There is another reason why he hasn't arrived yet."

Could she be that blind to the truth?

As there was a strong chance that the pigeon returned to the same gaming tables tonight to roost, he made a call on his mobile to his closest friend, drilled a finger into the speaker icon and laid the phone on the table.

"*Bonjour*," came Jean Paul's greeting.

"*Ciao*," Stefano replied. "Where are you?"

"Monte Carlo," his friend said. "Sun Casino to be precise. The high stakes poker game starts in less than an hour."

"Do you remember the young fisherman who sold me the old trawler a couple of weeks ago?" Stefano asked and locked gazes with Gemma.

"*Oui*. Cardone," he said. "He's here again and has just won five hundred thousand euros at the blackjack table. That win has certainly secured him an invitation to the game tonight."

Gemma shot to her feet. "No! Emilio doesn't have that kind of money. How could he think to take that risk?"

Stefano ruthlessly blocked her troubled image from his mind and spoke to Jean Paul. "In case you did not hear the lady, where did Cardone come by that much capital?"

"He has steadily won all day, the last round being the largest take yet."

Enough to pay the debt to Marinetti and then some, Stefano would wager. But the gambler's blood in Cardone lured him to increase it. To risk all. To ruin his sister?

"Has Cardone made any calls this evening?" Stefano asked.

"Not that I could tell. Although his phone did ring a while ago," Jean Paul said. "He answered it then promptly hung up."

Gemma's narrow shoulders lost a bit of their stiff edge to bow in as if on the verge of collapse.

What was the American saying? *No honor among thieves*?

Her brother knew full well she'd be waiting here with Stefano. He knew the consequences if she failed to make the payment tonight.

Her brother had left her to sink or swim.

Yes, he wanted the woman with a ravenous hunger.

Yes, he would have her.

But it wouldn't be to save her brother from ruin.

"Watch him," Stefano said, then ended that call and assessed his dinner companion.

Gemma's frantic gaze flicked over him. Her obvious pain was a gut punch he hadn't expected.

She had used his father. She'd caused his mamma pain. But the satisfaction he'd expected from besting her didn't come.

"You have less than an hour to meet the first loan payment," he reminded her. "Will you concede defeat now?"

She shook her head and he knew before she opened her mouth that she'd voice a protest. "The least you could have done was extend the deadline until morning when the banker is scheduled to give me his answer on my loan request. Cesare would have."

How dare she drag his papa into this argument! "I am sure you would have done your best to *persuade* Papa to let the debt ride longer. You have succeeded in draining his accounts to the extreme already!"

"I've done no such thing," she shot back.

"No? Then explain why my father transferred five hundred thousand euros into a private account bearing your name? What did you do with that money, plus all the monthly with-drawals he placed in your name?"

Her face turned whiter than Carrara marble. "I can't."

"Or won't," he said. "You were given enough money to build a five-star hotel that would gross millions. There will be no extensions. No second chances."

She shook her head and rubbed her temples. Her distress failed to stir his pity. She and her worthless brother had brought this on themselves. Now she'd suffer the consequences.

Revenge was in his grasp.

CHAPTER SIX

"I HATE you!" She tossed her napkin on the table, unwilling to sit here a moment longer with such a ruthless man. *Mio Dio*, what a nightmare!

"I could care less what you think of me, Miss Cardone."

She wasn't surprised for he was surely the most heartless man she'd ever had the displeasure of meeting. "Did you gain great satisfaction stripping my brother of his means to make a living?"

Stefano's muscular frame tensed, like a large cat waking from a nap and sensing trouble. "Your brother offered the vessel in order to remain in the game. If I hadn't paid his price, someone else would have."

She knew he was right, but facing the awful truth was crushing. Behind her back Emilio had been living the life of a playboy even though he didn't have the funds to squander. For how many months had he deceived them all?

Too many, she feared. She truly believed her brother had beaten his addiction over a year ago. But she'd been wrong.

She'd never dreamed he'd lie and hide the truth from her and in the process lose the business their father had worked and died for. And now because of his false promise to help her tonight, because she'd trusted her brother, she stood to lose her half of the inn!

"*Scusi*," she said and made for the door, her mind racing to find the swiftest means to reach Monte Carlo.

"Where are you going?"

"To my brother."

"Why? What do you hope to accomplish by going there?"

"To stop him from this gambling binge he's on." And if possible, claim what was due her before the dreaded deadline.

"He won't listen to you, *bella*."

He grabbed her arm and pulled her to him, his gaze darkly intense and pulsing with anger and vengeance and another emotion that was there and gone before she could recognize it. And then there was the power of his long, lean fingers snaked around her arm and the fire and energy arcing from him to her like a lightning storm, making her knees weak and her heart heavy.

Why did he have to be so ruthless?

He cupped her cheek in his palm and she blinked back sudden tears, for his tenderness mocked the animosity he held for her. "Even if you could reason with him, he's in a high stakes game that plays hard and fast."

She wasn't sure what that meant, but she knew she could only do one thing. Honor the promise she'd made to her parents. To Nonna.

"All the more reason for me to go there now."

She jerked from Stefano and ran from the room, hating that she drew attention to herself, hating that she didn't know how she could stop this avalanche of doom descending on her family.

Stefano caught up to her just as she reached the main room. As before he pressed a hand to the small of her back and she came up short, as if there was an invisible thread between them that only he controlled.

"How do you intend to get there at this hour?" he asked in a deceptively low calm voice.

"I don't know. A plane, perhaps."

"You will end up waiting for hours. The game could be over by then."

"Then I'll rent a car and drive the distance."

"Unacceptable."

They stepped outside and he snapped his fingers, sending the attendant rushing to fetch his car.

"I suppose you have a better idea?" she asked.

A darkening scowl crossed his features, giving him that fierce gladiator mien again. At that moment she believed him capable of conquering anything. Her brother. Her. The world.

"Let your brother sink or swim. It is over, *bella*. You can't change him and you can't meet the deadline. Accept it."

"I won't stand by and do nothing."

The tendons in his neck stood out and his dark eyes blazed with anger at her defiance. Not that she cared what he thought.

It was her family who would suffer.

But even if Stefano had any concept of family, he'd not care about the turmoil she suffered. She had to talk sense into her brother and get him help before he was in debt so deeply he'd never get out.

"I will not allow you to do this."

Gemma gaped at Stefano. Was he serious?

"You can't stop me."

She knew that was the wrong thing to say when his eyes darkened to that feral black again. But he held his thoughts and she suspected that was because they were surrounded by people.

But she knew a cauldron of anger boiled within him. Anger at her brother, at her. At his father?

It was the reason why that puzzled her.

Then she recalled what had started this all. He'd mentioned the vast sum Cesare had spent the past year. Money he'd used for his daughter's care as well as the generous gift he'd insisted she have.

Her nest egg for a better tomorrow though she'd spent it all on the inn. Her nonna had lived long enough in squalor.

Gemma wasn't about to let her continue to do so, not when she finally had the means to make the necessary repairs. If Cesare hadn't needed her, she would have returned to Manarolo and taken over the inn herself. It wasn't as if she'd be usurping her sister-in-law's duties!

But she couldn't tell Stefano any of that, for to do so would reveal the secret she'd swore to hold for Cesare. Now seeing how little regard Stefano held for family, she didn't dare trust him with the truth.

"You can't meet the deadline for the loan," he said as he escorted her to his car. "Which means I will own your half of the inn. If you hope to negotiate a means to regain the title, you would be wise to do as I tell you to do."

Gemma's heart stuttered, aware that domineering threat wasn't a mere boast. But was he serious about giving her a chance to regain her half of the inn? "What are you suggesting?"

"We'll discuss it later." He motioned for her to get in the car, his expression carefully devoid of emotion again. "You want to go to Monte Carlo tonight, then I will take you."

"Then neither of us will be back at work in the morning," she said as she got in the car.

"Work can wait."

In moments he'd slid behind the wheel and cut into traffic with the expertise of a Formula 1 driver and she realized he was dead serious.

She didn't relish the idea of racing over the mountains in

the middle of the night with Stefano Marinetti. But she couldn't waste another second reaching her brother, either.

"How long will it take to drive there?"

"Too long. We are taking my helicopter."

He couldn't be serious.

But as he turned onto the main road and sped back toward the shipyard, she knew that Stefano Marinetti wasn't jesting.

An hour later, Stefano set down the helicopter in the executive heliport at Monte Carlo. Gemma hadn't said a word since they'd lifted off, even though he'd fitted her with earphones.

But then he hadn't felt obliged to strike up a conversation, either. For one thing, the night-flight had demanded all his concentration. For another he didn't trust himself to remain impassive when the very air they breathed pulsed with tension.

Though he'd expected it, he still found it galling that she'd asked for an extension on the damned loan. "Cesare would've granted it," she'd said, and he was certain she was right.

That was all the reminder he'd needed to believe that she'd appeal to his father as soon as she could. She'd get back in Cesare's good graces and his bed.

But the possibility of her taking her position further loomed large before him, especially now that she stood to lose her shares of the inn. Marriage would cement her place in his father's life and grant her the power to do whatever the hell she wished with what little money remained.

And considering her devotion to her brother, that money would likely find its way to Monte Carlo.

No, he couldn't let her near his father. Instead he must make a more attractive proposition to her, and he must give her little chance to refuse.

As soon as it was safe to exit the helicopter, he hurried her across the helipad and into the waiting limo. His blood heated from the light scent that was uniquely hers and the excitement that crackled in the air. From the fact that when this nasty business was concluded here, he and Gemma would form a new arrangement.

That she'd be his.

Flashes of lights confirmed the paparazzi were out in force, leading him to believe that more celebrities than usual were partaking of the games of chance or just visiting on the chance to be noticed partying among the ultrarich.

He'd never found this jet-set lifestyle appealing. Staying on the cutting edge of his business and promoting it to its fullest kept him on the go. Unlike a good number of his contemporaries, he preferred to celebrate his successes with a select few or in private with a beautiful woman.

Like Gemma?

He shoved that thought from his mind and concentrated on what had brought him here tonight. Gemma.

How ironic that just two weeks ago Jean Paul had goaded him to come gamble. Buying Cardone's old trawler had made it worth his time.

And now?

The last text message he'd received from Jean Paul hinted at a repeat of the last time he'd been pitted against Cardone. Only this victory tonight would be over Gemma.

It would be all the sweeter. When she saw her brother fail this time, she'd have no choice but to accept what Stefano offered. No choice at all.

"How in the world will I find Emilio here?" Gemma asked, her voice so low he wondered if she was talking to herself.

The hand he had pressed to her spine slid to her side—all to get a better hold on her as they wended their way through this throng. It had nothing to do with offering her comfort for the turmoil she'd face in the next hour. Nothing!

"Cardone is in the poker room engaged in a high stakes game," he said. "He has lost the last two hands."

"How do you know that?" she asked.

"My friend sent me a message some time ago," he said.

She stopped and stared at him. "Did you hire your friend to gamble against Emilio?"

"No, Jean Paul is a billionaire with a talent and desire to gamble on his off time." He didn't bother to mention Jean Paul was a celebrated Formula 1 driver, for what was the point?

"Come. We'll join the audience, but you must remain quiet," he said. "Any disruption will have you removed."

She glared at him for the longest time with nothing short of hatred. With a huff, she turned and strode down the hall, back impossibly rigid.

Fine. He would rather she hate him; he could deal with that better than coping with the desire and empathy she'd stirred to life in him earlier. If she raised a ruckus, she'd find herself hustled from the room.

It would only make the tension between them all the more stronger later when they sat down to business. Yes, they were waging their own high stakes games. But he would win.

He could make her want him. He could make her wild with desire. He would have his vengeance!

Because he intended to blackmail her into his bed? His cheeks burned, a rarity to be sure.

But for all his shrewd business sense, he'd never mistreated a woman in his life. Never! Not even the one he'd brought home to meet his parents and who set her sights on his brother.

But that anger that always roared to life failed to come.

In its place was a new emotion. Stronger. More volatile.

This business between him and Gemma had meaning. This fired his blood.

This was archaic thinking. It was something he'd never done and never thought to do with a woman.

But he couldn't back down. Not now. Not when the scent of her filled his senses, when the brief kiss they'd shared inflamed his desire.

"Marinetti," he told the guard at the door.

The man nodded and stepped aside without a word.

Gemma hesitated, but Stefano's hand to her back hurried her inside. A row of plush chairs cast in shadow faced the tables.

She eased onto a chair and stared at him with eyes that were too huge and too filled with an emotion he couldn't grasp. The deep sense of hurt that dimmed her eyes charged the tension-filled air and raised the hair at his nape.

"Call," said the Russian mogul playing against Cardone.

The last chips where thrust forward. The cards revealed. Cardone lost.

She looked at Stefano and asked in a whisper, "Is it over?"

He nodded in answer, and her narrow shoulders bowed. In fact her entire body seemed to cave in on itself.

Damn her brother for doing this to her. Then he damned himself for letting her get to him. For wanting to take her in his arms and comfort her.

"All players must purchase the required chips before the start of the next game."

Cardone pushed from the table and stalked to the bank, a trip he'd undoubtedly made countless times. "I have title to property. Will you take that as surety for a stake in the next game?"

"Yes, if you have it with you."

"What is he doing?" Gemma said, her tension so acute Stefano felt it abrading his nerves.

Cardone produced a document and handed it to the bank. "The inn on Manarolo is in good condition and makes a modest profit."

The bank took the paper. "One moment to verify this, sir."

"No! He doesn't own the inn." She rushed to her brother, drawing all eyes to her.

Stefano followed on her heels, wanting to believe that Gemma had lied all along about the ownership of the inn. But her reaction was too genuine to be staged.

She was shocked by her brother's actions to the point of hysteria.

Cardone whirled on her then, eyes widening with surprise before narrowing in anger. "What are you doing here?"

"Stopping you from making a mistake," she said. "How did you get Nonna's shares of the inn?"

Her brother let out a smug laugh. "Nonna is already heart-broken that you lost your half of the inn to Marinetti."

"You told her about that?" she asked, her voice dropping to a choked whisper.

"Of course. She signed over her half of the inn to me, the family who has stayed by her side this past year."

"The family who is about to gamble away our heritage!" She clasped trembling hands over her mouth and stared at her brother as if he were a stranger. "What are you thinking? The inn is your home. It's our family's livelihood. You live there. Your wife works with Nonna and affords you a modest income off the guests."

"Peasant wages," Cardone spat. "I want more for my family and myself." He flicked a damning glower at Stefano. "I want the kind of life your rich boss enjoys."

"Then work for it!"

"Trust me in this, *mio serella*," Cardone said to Gemma,

the endearment sounding false to Stefano's ears. "When I win this pot you'll never have to bow and scrape for a *milionario* again," he said, inclining his head Stefano's way. "You would be independently wealthy."

"You can't risk our home," she said, and Stefano realized the source of her fear.

He owned her shares now, and if her brother sold his, then their family would be cast out on the street. The inn that had been handed down from generation to generation would be lost.

Cardone grasped Gemma's upper arms and drew her close. Her startled gasp touched something inside Stefano, something that smacked of jealousy. Something that spurred him to protect her any way he could.

He just barely stayed the urge to shove Cardone aside and take Gemma into *his* arms. Just barely. And that admission enraged him for he had just proven he was no better than his father around her.

"Your home," Cardone repeated, the biting sarcasm in his voice hushing those in the room again. "You would do anything to hold on to that crumbling pile of stones, even sell yourself to an old man."

"Apologize to the lady," Stefano said, barely restraining himself from physically hauling Cardone outside and laying into him.

Never mind he had accused Gemma of the same thing. He had not voiced such crudities in public.

"Defending her?" Cardone asked, setting his sister aside. "In this attack? *Sì*."

Which made no sense because Stefano had wanted to publicly humiliate her. He'd wanted to ruin her and recover as much of his father's property and money as he could.

Cardone sneered at Gemma. "You go from doting on one Marinetti to the other and turn your back on your brother."

"You don't want my help. You just want what money I can spare so you can toss it away on the turn of a card."

She turned to Stefano but didn't look him in the eyes, seeming shamed and weary and oh so vulnerable. "Please, take me away from here. I can't bear to watch anymore."

This was his chance to walk away and complete her humiliation. This was the time to put her in her place once and for all and defend his family's honor.

Honor.

To an Italian, honor was everything. But the timing felt wrong. This wasn't the place or time.

"The title is verified," the bank said to Cardone.

"Take her away from here," Cardone said, then turned to accept the casino's offer.

Nobody noticed Gemma's distress and obvious depression. Nobody but Stefano.

"I'll give you five hundred thousand euros for the title," Stefano said, doing this for himself for he had no desire to have a stranger as his partner.

It had nothing to do with Gemma's crushing defeat. Nothing to do with revenge. He did not want to feel anything for this woman but disgust. She'd all but stolen from his father, yet she portrayed the injured party so well now that he almost sympathized with her.

Cardone smirked and snatched the title from the bank. "I accept your offer, Marinetti."

"Think of what this will do to Nonna," Gemma said, her voice rough with emotion now.

But Cardone merely shrugged. "Perhaps the new owner will allow her to stay on there, if given the proper incentives."

And again Stefano wanted to throttle the man for his crude innuendoes hurled at Gemma in public. It went without saying that the old woman could live out her days in her home. But he refused to comment now.

Far too much had been said already.

A quiet hum resumed in the room with gamblers taking their places for the next game. He caught the questioning look in his friend's eye, but didn't attempt to engage in conversation.

This wasn't the time.

He wanted out of here before he truly did lose his temper with Cardone. Just one more insult to Gemma was all it would take, and wasn't that a thorn for Stefano to contend with?

The transaction went swiftly with Cardone signing his name with a flourish and Gemma standing stiff and solemn beside Stefano.

He tucked the title in his suit pocket then pressed a hand to her back. "It is time to leave, *bella*."

She simply nodded and walked out with her head high.

He caught himself admiring her pride in the face of such adversity.

It was over. He owned the inn now.

But he felt no victory. Not yet.

He controlled what she wanted most. The inn. The question was what would she agree to do to gain back the title.

CHAPTER SEVEN

SHE shouldn't have left Monte Carlo with Stefano. She should've taken the train back home.

Home.

She didn't have a home any longer, just a flat in Viareggio. She'd let her nonna down in the worst possible way.

What would happen next?

Gemma had to ask Stefano about his plans for the inn. For if he intended to sell it, there was the slim chance she could still secure a loan from the bank.

It was a slim thread to hang onto as she sat beside him in the helicopter, the lights of the casino fading as they flew out over the Ligurian Sea that lay black and fathomless at night. If only that emotionally draining scene with Emilio in the poker room would diminish as well.

But it didn't. It remained clear and garish.

She'd failed to help her brother. In fact she didn't know how to reach him anymore. She didn't know if she had the heart to try, and that only heaped more guilt on her already tired shoulders.

Emilio knew exactly what she'd done to get the money to refurbish the inn, yet he twisted the truth into something ugly.

He insinuated that she had been Cesare's mistress and that she was now Stefano's lover.

She hadn't even had the heart to deny it for what good would it have done? Stefano hadn't said anything in his defense, either, just stared at her with those dark, smoldering eyes like he had right before he'd kissed her.

Mio Dio, even hours later she could still taste him on her tongue. Still feel the steely strength in the arms that had held her close. Still remember the evidence of his desire against her belly.

Oh, yes, they had given the gossips plenty of fodder to feed on this night. She just hoped news of it wouldn't reach Cesare soon.

The day for his open-heart surgery had arrived. The last thing he needed was the stress caused by these vicious lies.

Stress.

Her life was a total disaster now. She'd never felt this adrift. This separated from everything she'd known and loved and trusted.

She wanted to know what Stefano's plans were for the inn. But even with the headphones, the roar of the blades dissuaded conversation.

So she held her thoughts and fears to herself and settled in for the long ride back to Viareggio. That thought had barely crossed her mind when she spotted the lights of a big ship dead ahead. The helicopter circled it once and then began descending.

Her mind ran away with dire reasons why Stefano would set down in the middle of the sea. And wasn't this dangerous to attempt at night?

Never mind he was landing on a small cruise ship. He was doing so nearly blind at night.

Before she could work herself into a full-blown panic, he'd

landed the helicopter. Her heart stopped its frantic pounding so she could hear him speaking to someone over his radio.

She immediately thought of Cesare. "Is something wrong?" she asked before they both removed their headphones.

"It is late and I didn't wish to fly back to Viareggio tonight when my yacht was so close by."

She stared out on the deck of the large ship. "This huge boat is yours?"

He slid her a devilish grin that had her seeing him as a desirable man instead of the man who'd just gained control of all she held dear. A very handsome man with an odd glint in his eyes that roused her suspicions.

If he thought she'd tumble into bed with him now, he was sorely mistaken. There had to be plenty of rooms on board. Hopefully there was one far from his domain.

"This is the starship of my new fleet," he said with pride ringing clear in his tone. "I can work from here as easily as I can on land."

"Have you done that often?" she said in an attempt to make idle conversation.

"Many times of late. Come."

He stepped from the helicopter and rounded it to assist her down. An odd thing to do since there were plenty of men who had jumped to attend to the helicopter and its billionaire pilot.

A refreshing breeze greeted her as she crossed the deck with her hand tightly clasped in Stefano's. Possessive. Sensual.

The last sensation thrummed her nerves in an erotic melody she couldn't deny. She didn't want to feel anything toward him but animosity.

Though she was helpless to stop the swift stab of desire, hell would surely freeze over before she acted upon it. With that thought in mind, she was able to draw a decent breath as he led her belowdecks.

If Gemma didn't know better, she'd swear she'd just entered a sunken palace. Marble floors and pillars, plush Brussels carpets that her feet sank into, crystal light fixtures that caught the light and reflected it back in a rich rainbow of color.

Servants rushed to attend to Stefano's needs but he waved them off. "I need nothing more tonight," he said as he tugged Gemma down a hall and into a large suite.

"It's gorgeous," she said as she took in the massive stateroom.

The lighting was subdued. The furnishing modern yet masculinely opulent.

"This is the salon where we meet clients." He crossed to a bar. "May I get you something?"

This was one of those occasions when she needed alcohol. "Chianti, please."

Stefano obliged and handed her a glass. "I imagine you are close to exhaustion."

"It's been an extremely taxing day."

He nodded agreement. "But there is one more bit of business I wish to discuss now."

The inn. She was sure of it.

He had her where he could punish and torment her and they both knew it. It was a matter of how much blood he wanted from her for not confiding in her personal affairs.

She drank her wine too fast and felt a wave of dizziness engulf her. "Very well," she said in her most businesslike tone. "What is it that is so urgent?"

"I gather the inn means a great deal to you."

"More than it could possibly mean to you. I want the opportunity to buy it back," she said, her chin lifting for the argument she was sure would come.

"Fine," he said so quickly she nearly reeled. "I have no wish to delve into the hotel business at any level."

"Then why did you buy Emilio's shares?" she asked.

He poured an equal amount of wine in his glass and took a sip. "Because I didn't want a third party to have any say over my plans for the inn."

His answer left her more confused than before. "You just said you had no wish to manage an inn."

"I don't. But I didn't want to divide the shares, either."

A fact she appreciated even though it forced her to appeal to him solely now. "Then do you agree to sell the inn to me?"

His firm lips curved into that wicked smile again. "Selling is a lengthy process I'd prefer avoiding."

"I planned to get a loan—"

He raised a hand and she fell silent. "I don't want money, *bella*. I want you."

"What do you mean?" she asked, though she feared she knew where this was leading.

"I want you to be my mistress."

She set the glass down though she was tempted to hurl it at his hard head. "I won't prostitute myself for you or anyone."

One devilishly dark eyebrow lifted in mock questioning. "Not even for sole ownership of your inn on Manarolo?"

Damn him! "I can get a loan and pay you—"

"Don't bother," he said. "You will not work for Marinetti beyond another month."

"You're firing me?"

He shrugged. "I am extending you one offer, *bella*. In addition to your duties as my personal secretary, I want you to be my mistress for one month."

"You're vile."

"Think what you like. In exchange for your companionship for one month, I'll give you the title to the inn on Manarolo free and clear."

She hadn't thought she could hate him more than she did at this second, but a fury like she'd never felt before surged through her. She wanted to pummel his chest, kick him. She wanted to walk out of his life and never look back.

But he had her in a vulnerable position.

Unless she was willing to break her promise to Cesare, or see her inn sold to a stranger and her nonna displaced, she had no choice but to agree to Stefano's outrageous demands. The fact that her body did respond to the power and erotic pulse of his was moot—and if she told herself that enough, just maybe she'd believe it.

The cold fact remained that he was dangling the prize before her eyes. All she had to do to gain her heart's desire was be his mistress.

She wouldn't have to like it. She just had to lay there and suffer his touch for a month.

As if his touch would bring her anything but pleasure the likes she'd never known before!

"I want it in writing," she said, disgusted her voice trembled. "I won't sleep with you until then."

A muscle tensed in his lean cheek and she braced herself for an argument. "Agreed. It is after all a solid business proposition."

It was a personal proposition to settle a vendetta, to bend her to his will because he simply could. Because he believed she had been his father's mistress first and had bled Cesare of his fortune. What would happen when the truth did come out?

Truths, she amended.

She'd never been with a man before, and he was sure to realize that. How long could she put him off?

Not long, she feared. What in the world would she tell him then regarding the jaunts to Milan?

He set his glass down and strode toward her, nudging her chin up with a finger that sent a new wave of awareness crashing through her. She hated that her body responded so readily to him.

"You look dead on your feet. Come, let me show you to your stateroom." He guided her across the salon with a hand to her back, a hand that left her burning hot as if he'd left his brand on her skin.

She broke contact with him as soon as she walked into the suite. But the effort drained her and the soft lighting, the quiet, all tempted her to curl up on the first sofa she came to and sleep.

But before she did, she had to appease the final thing that would rob her of rest. "Have you spoken with your father?"

His shoulders snapped taut for a moment, as if her query had been a stinging lash. "I talked with his nurse earlier. He's resting and his surgery is scheduled for tomorrow."

"I gather you've instructed your crew to travel through the night," she said.

"They have their orders."

He pushed through double doors into a large bedroom that was dominated by a sumptuous bed. "The rooms are well stocked for impromptu visits. I trust you will find everything you need."

Did he entertain off-the-cuff often? Or was he speaking of his feminine conquests and the provisions he kept on hand for them?

Jealousy slammed into her, blocking everything but the fact that she couldn't bear to envision Stefano with anyone else. He was the last man she dreamed of making love with, and yet the only man who had invaded her dreams with lusty temptations and promises of forbidden pleasure.

Would reality prove half as wonderful?

"I'm sure I'll manage," she said, too weary to drum up genuine annoyance at him at this point.

What's done was done.

"If you require anything, my suite is right across the salon," he said, seeming in no hurry to leave her quarters.

His tie hung loose around the strong column of his neck. He'd unbuttoned his shirt, revealing a teasing glimpse of his sculpted chest dusted with black hair.

The contrast between stark white shirt and deeply tanned olive skin fascinated her. She'd spent her life around fishermen whose skin had baked a dark brown working in the sun. Her papa had had skin like leather.

Not so for Stefano. His skin looked smooth and soft, stretching taut over hard, unyielding muscles. Soon she'd know what he looked like without clothes. She'd feel that strong hard body moving on hers.

She clasped her hands together to still their trembling. And instantly noticed something very wrong.

"No!" She stared at her ring finger. Her *bare* ring finger.

"*Bella*, what troubles you?" he asked, his voice a rich baritone that stroked over her skin and left her trembling.

"My ring," she said, and quickly described the marquise cut aquamarine flanked by two tiny diamonds that matched her necklace. "I've lost it somewhere."

"I'll have the servants search the boat and helicopter for it," he said "*D'accordo?*"

She nodded, even though it was not okay. Her papa had given her that ring when she'd gotten her degree. Losing it was like losing her papa all over again.

She hugged her waist when she ached for someone to hold her. No, not someone. Stefano.

She'd lost too much. Her parents. The inn. And now Cesare's life hung in the balance.

"I would like to accompany you to the hospital tomorrow," she said, desperately needing to see the older man.

Again that abrupt tightening of his shoulders and back. "The doctors have stressed he is not to think of work."

"I won't mention the shipyard except to say all is fine," she promised, not about to be dismissed so easily. "Please. I am worried about Cesare and will be a nervous wreck waiting at the office for news."

"Of course." His smile was tight, and a hardened glint sparked his eyes now. Anger?

Yes, he was likely annoyed that she'd insisted on coming to the hospital. He must know he couldn't stop her, that her being there was simply a show of support.

She was first and foremost Cesare's personal secretary! This unsavory agreement she made with Stefano fell below that—as he'd said, it was simply business.

"Sleep," he said. "I can promise you that you won't get much rest tomorrow night."

And with that predictive remark he was gone.

She stared at the closed door a long moment, but the subdued light and luxurious bed called to her. He was right. She needed rest.

Gemma found a silk gown in the bureau, one of a dozen that still had tags on them. A good deal of her pique drained away knowing she wouldn't be wearing his lover's castoffs.

Yes, morning would come far too soon, she thought as she crawled into bed and doused the light. She sank into the down topper and sighed.

All she needed was a few hours' sleep.

But she couldn't close her eyes for when she did, she saw

Stefano's arrogant face and the dark desire that lit his eyes, which stirred an unsettling restlessness within her. So she paced the large bedroom in the velvet hush of night and prayed for exhaustion to overtake her.

How appropriate that he was as difficult to remove from her thoughts as he was from her life! When her mind grew too crowded with imaginings of what he expected of a mistress, she peeked out into the salon.

It was empty. All was quiet, and why shouldn't it be since it was nearly four o'clock in the morning.

Gemma slipped into the salon and paused, her brief silk nightgown cool against her bare skin. She debated going back to find a robe or coverlet, then decided not to bother.

She was alone here. Stefano was asleep, and hopefully if she paced between the porthole and exterior door another thirty minutes she'd grow too weary to keep her eyes open, too.

"You should be in bed," Stefano said, his deep voice reaching her from the dark recesses of the room.

She stopped and stared at him bathed in shadows. How long had he been standing there watching her?

"I couldn't sleep," she said. "A problem I've had for years."

"Does nothing help?"

"If I grow tired enough from pacing and fretting, I will usually fall asleep for several hours."

"You need a better diversion than pacing."

She was tired and cranky and in no mood to spar with Stefano tonight. "What do you suggest?"

"*Facciamo l'amore.*"

Making love was *not* a good idea, not without her new contract in hand.

"We agreed to begin tomorrow night."

One broad, masculine shoulder lifted in a lazy shrug, and

as the faint moonlight played over his olive skin she realized he wasn't wearing a shirt. Her throat went tight as her gaze lowered, admiring his taut belly ribbed with muscle, lean hips that would make a god proud and the evidence of his desire that jutted hard and long toward her.

Gemma's legs turned to jelly, refusing to support her. Or maybe the heat from his gaze and the fire now sparking to life within her melted whatever usually held her upright.

She managed a weak, "Oh," as she crumbled.

But she never hit the floor.

No, Stefano moved like lightning to catch her up against him. Gemma pushed against his chest, but the effort was halfhearted.

Her palms skimmed that unyielding masculine wall she'd longed to touch and she simply forgot how to breathe.

He was hot and strong and oh so sexy. Even in the dim light she could see his eyes weren't a solid brown but dusted with flecks of gold.

Right now those specks were molten, melting any reservation that dared to cross her mind. Not that much was crossing her mind except how wonderful it felt to be held this close to this man.

"I can't let you do this," she said, the words tumbling from her in a breathy whisper as she realized that he was going to kiss her.

Or was she simply seeing what she wanted to see?

The seductive slant of his smile warmed her more than a full sun. "Why try to stop what we both want?"

His mouth captured hers, the kiss long and deep and drugging. Passion sang through her veins in a virtuoso's concerto, bringing tears to her eyes for the sheer beauty and power that flowed from him into her.

She didn't know how a kiss could muddle her so, but she

was lost in his embrace, in this moment. He pressed her into the bed without breaking the kiss and she started. How had he carried her to her bedroom without her being aware of it?

Then the question was lost as he stroked her arms, her back, her breasts, taking his time with each. The glide of her silk gown was a barrier she loathed and an aphrodisiac that heightened her pleasure.

Oh, and what pleasure he gave!

His mouth moved over hers with ravenous passion and she trembled, starving for more. Each bold thrust of his tongue parried with hers sent an answering throb to the very core of her.

She writhed against him, wanting something she could only imagine. It was as if she'd slumbered all her life and just came awake now.

"Kiss me, *bella*," he murmured against her lips. "Kiss me like you want to."

Dare she? Her experience was laughable, but her desire was great.

Her small hands glided up his bare chest, awed and emboldened by the telling tremors that passed from this tall, muscular man into her. His hands weren't passive, either, and those long fingers gliding over her sensitized skin adored and teased in turn. How could she have thought this man hard and cruel?

They were chest to breast, yet she ached to be closer. She hooked her legs around his lean hips, the movement pressing her sex to the hard length of his.

The silk of her gown sheathed his penis, yet each shift of their bodies created a delicious friction that shocked and emboldened her. She wanted skin on skin, wanting to know this man as intimately as a woman could.

The desire was bold and totally unlike her. Yet she felt no shame. Just want.

Her mouth played over his, treating him to the same sensual torment he'd afforded her. A deep moan of satisfaction rumbled from him, melding with the blissful sighs she could no longer hold back.

"You are made for loving," he said, his lips trailing over skin he'd just bared.

Her skin pebbled under his knowing touch, but old promises and new fears threatened to dampen her amorous mood. He made a growling sound of protest and continued his exploration of her neck, her breasts.

"You deserve a lifetime of amorous pleasure, *mio caro*."

She tried to summon up anger that Stefano only wanted an affair with her. But his mouth settled over one bare nipple and a maelstrom of new sensations exploded within her.

What would be quickly faded into oblivion. Her life suddenly hinged on this sensual fever he ignited in her.

She arched against him and breathed a sigh of relief when he rid her of her gown, the sound of tearing silk more erotic than she could have imagined.

She gloried in those strong, masculine hands that played over her skin, amazed that he knew what she liked, what she craved, more than she knew herself.

In this there were no barriers between them. At least not physical ones.

They were a man and woman in the throes of a passion that was far too intense for her to imagine. *Mio Dio*, if Stefano was that passionately aggressive for an entire month, she'd never purge him from her mind.

No, don't think on those terms! Don't think of falling in love with Stefano.

But how could she not imagine giving her heart to this man when he whispered a litany of love words in her ear. When he made her feel desirable and wanted and loved.

"*Bella*," he breathed as his sex filled her.

She gasped more from surprise and pressure than any pain that she'd been warned she'd feel this first time with a man. No, any pain she felt was in her mind—for what could never be between them.

He went still, his dark eyes registering a moment's shock as well. And she knew that he recognized she'd been a virgin.

She could almost read the second doubts he was warring with himself. The surprise that she wasn't what he'd accused her of being.

She arched against him. "Please, don't stop."

His expression became more intense, more possessive. Then his mouth captured hers in a long, drugging kiss that left her awash in pleasure and need.

She raked her fingers down his back and melted against him, reveling in the new sensations. So this was how it felt to be joined to a man.

She hadn't imagined she'd feel so free. That this moment would feel so right.

Stefano cupped her face in his palms and locked gazes with her, and she marveled that even in the dim light she saw her need reflected in his dark eyes. "You are mine now. Do you understand?"

She nodded, but she refused to read anything into that arrogant comment besides the fact she was now his mistress.

Then he sank into her fully and withdrew before she could catch her breath, only to do it again and again. His mouth dipped to hers and she met him midway, the kiss going as wild and frenzied as his thrusts.

There were no more words, just an explosion of sensations and pleasures that their bodies understood.

She matched his strong, sure movements, clinging to him in helpless abandon. The sensations building within her were too huge, nearly too intense to bear. Just as she feared she'd faint from the sheer joy of finding completion in his arms, they climaxed together.

Gemma had heard the saying of two becoming one, but she hadn't understood what it meant until now. She felt his heart beat in every pore in her body, felt the tension and power of the man rippling through her in sultry waves.

He rolled to his side and took her with him, still inside her, still holding her close to his heart. She nestled against the solid wall of his chest, his heartbeat loud and steady against her ear.

He was as much a part of her as she of him. She felt branded by his touch, his possession. She felt wanted and desirous and loved.

A delicious, drowsy warmth spread over her. She yawned, her last coherent thought was she'd be content to spend every night just like this.

This was heaven.

This was a delicious dream from which she never wanted to awaken. But she knew before she closed her eyes that it would end all too soon.

For the morning he was sure to pepper her with questions that she still couldn't answer.

The *whomp-whomp* of the helicopter snapped Gemma from her euphoric dream. She lay in the bed a tense moment, disoriented by the splendor surrounding her.

The yacht.

Stefano.

This bed where they'd made love last night.

His masculine, spicy scent that lingered on the sheets and her skin. The tenderness of her breasts and the flesh between her legs.

She reached to his side. The sheet and pillow were cool. Not even an indentation remained to prove he'd been here.

The helicopter!

She bounded from the bed and winced, her body protesting the sudden movement in the wake of the erotic pleasure she'd gained last night. Her gown lay in a wad of torn silk on the floor.

Impatiently she tore through the closet to find a thick velour wrapper. She bundled up in it and rushed into the salon, still feeling cold inside.

A maid started from straightening the room. "*Scusi.*"

Gemma shrugged aside the woman's apology. "Where is Stefano?"

The maid looked to the window. "He left."

"In the helicopter?"

"*Sì.* May I bring your breakfast?"

Gemma shook her head and rushed out the door. She paused a second to get her bearings then darted down the hall toward the large room at the end.

Gaining the upper deck proved easy enough, but she was too late to stop Stefano or even catch his attention. Not that he'd have paid her any heed anyway.

No, he'd loved her to distraction last night and then left her here on his yacht this morning while he went to the hospital to be with Cesare. He'd lied to her!

The reason was clear to her. He didn't trust her to stay away as he'd asked. He'd brought her here last night to ensure she'd not be able to get to land until *he* decreed it so. The yacht was so far at sea she couldn't even see land!

Gemma stormed back to her stateroom and slammed the

door. If he'd lied about this, could she trust him to keep his promise regarding the inn?

A cold emptiness expanded in her, freezing any pleasure she'd felt in his arms. The suite where she'd made such passionate love with Stefano now felt like a silken prison.

You are mine now, he'd said.

But he hadn't meant it in the sense of them being closer as a couple. No, it had been a possessive comment and nothing more.

He had her under his thumb. Or so he thought.

She was a fisherman's daughter. She knew the sea and these people. Somehow she'd find a way to get back to Italy.

Gemma *had* to return today to see Cesare, if only to assure herself he was healing after his surgery. Then she must travel to Milan for there was a little girl waiting impatiently for her visit. And what would she tell her about Cesare's absence?

The truth.

It'd been hidden long enough.

CHAPTER EIGHT

STEFANO paced the near empty waiting room and damned the time that seemed to crawl by—unlike this morning which had flown by in a rush. He'd not wanted to leave Gemma's side. He'd wanted to get lost in her lush body again.

She'd been a virgin. *Virgin*!

If not for his strong will, he'd have shaken her awake at dawn and demanded to know what the hell she and his papa had been doing all those weekends in Milan. But he didn't have the time to delve into it now.

And he didn't trust her to do as he ordered once they reached land. He didn't want to hear any more of her lies. No, he wanted to hear his papa's side of this now.

But he'd gotten to the hospital too late thanks to his reluctance at tearing himself from Gemma and then a traffic snarl after he landed in Viareggio.

Now he would have to wait for his papa to recover before he could get answers. That wasn't something he was even marginally good at doing.

"Stefano, please sit," his aunt had said, her usually radiant face looking haggard. "You are making me nervous with your endless pacing."

Maledizione! He certainly didn't wish to cause anyone any more grief.

He plopped on the stiff chair beside her and stretched his long legs out. "My apologies. You know patience isn't one of my strong suits."

"*Sì*, I know. But I also know my nephew and recognize when something is deeply troubling him."

"It has been a long morning without word how Papa is doing."

She clamped a hand on his arm and her tension vibrated into him. "Did you expect them to stop the surgery and deliver a report?"

"No, nothing like that."

"What is troubling you, Stefano?" his aunt asked.

Gemma. She invaded his thoughts. Sweet, beguiling Gemma. Sweet, *innocent* Gemma.

But he couldn't tell his papa's sister that. Not now when her stress was palpable for she would ask questions that he didn't wish to address, either. He sure as hell couldn't tell her he'd blackmailed his papa's secretary into his bed!

"There are things at Marinetti that require my attention today," he said.

She stared at him through narrowed eyes. "What about the secretary? Have you dismissed her yet?"

He heaved a sigh, wishing his mamma hadn't told her sister-in-law about Cesare's infidelity. Wishing to hell his mamma hadn't told him her suspicions at all.

"No. It is more complicated than I thought."

The color drained from her face as she pressed a hand to her generous bosom. "*Addio*! Please tell me this woman is not with child."

"Nothing of the sort," he said, and hoped to hell that proved true.

Maledizione! He hadn't used protection.

He hadn't thought it was necessary since she was his father's mistress.

Except she wasn't. He only hoped she was on the pill or used some type of birth control. But how likely was a virgin to do that?

Stefano drove his fingers through his hair and called himself ten kinds of an ass. Taking Gemma's virginity had robbed him of the vengeance he'd sought. It changed everything that he'd planned to do with her.

It forced him to reassess her role in his life and his future. He wanted to blame her for lying to him, except in this she'd told the truth. She wasn't his father's mistress—she was his by coercion.

Imbecile!

He'd never bedded a virgin before. Never wanted to.

He didn't want to think that he could have fathered a child with Gemma. He didn't want to think of her at all.

But as the day wore on and his worry for his papa increased, his thoughts continued to turn to Gemma. In his bed. Loving her and knowing that he was the first man to introduce her to sex.

Her sweet scent filled his head. He hungered for another taste of her honeyed mouth. To suckle the pert breasts until the rosy nipples budded on his tongue. To settle between her soft thighs and sup at the erotic essence of her, to drive her wild with ecstasy before covering her and making them one.

Unbidden came an overwhelming swell of possessiveness. She was his now. *His*.

Up until the time he took her virginity, he'd not been tied to her. He could have sent her on her way without repercussions.

He should never have set out to ruin her for in doing so he'd only tangled their lives together.

There was no going back.

He couldn't walk away. He *wouldn't* desert her until he knew if she carried his child.

What was done was done. If his seed grew in her, he'd accept his responsibility. He'd marry her without hesitation.

And if there was no child?

Stefano would honor the agreement they'd made for thirty days. Then he'd let her go.

By then this fierce possessiveness he felt toward her would have waned. He wouldn't be filled with rage over the thought of her moving on to a new lover. Of marrying one day. Of having children.

"I do not like that she is still on the payroll," his aunt said. "Your mamma's memory deserves more respect than that."

He heaved a sigh, vexed that his aunt was still brooding about Gemma. He certainly couldn't let his aunt go on believing the worst of Gemma but he did not relish telling her the truth, either.

"Mamma was mistaken about her," he said.

His aunt gaped at him. "Do not tell me she has woven you around her finger as well?"

He refused to dignify that with a denial and settled on facts instead. "Gemma Cardone wasn't Papa's lover."

"I suppose she told you that."

"She did and I refused to believe her."

"So what changed your mind?"

He shifted uneasily and made a cutting movement with his hand. "I was her first lover."

An awful quiet echoed in the waiting room to set his nerves on edge. "When?"

"This is not the time to discuss such things," he reminded his aunt when a couple entered the room and crossed to the chairs on the other side.

"Now is the perfect time," she said in a voice pitched low. "Tell me how long you've *known* this woman."

"We spent last night on the yacht." And in case his aunt had any doubts what he meant, he added, "In the same bed. She hadn't known any man before me."

She treated him to a long, assessing look before spitting out a torrent of curses directed at the male of the species. "You are sure of this?"

"Positive," he said. "She is Papa's personal secretary. That is all."

Yet even as he said it he knew Gemma was more to his father than that. There were the unexplained weekends spent in Milan and the small fortune that Cesare had given Gemma.

A man didn't hand over that kind of money to a stranger unless there was a very good reason. Gemma had never offered an explanation for her good fortune. She couldn't even look him in the eyes when the subject was brought up.

Stefano knew she was hiding something that involved her and his father. But what?

He'd visited Milan shortly after his mamma had voiced her suspicions about his papa straying, but all he'd discovered was that his papa and Gemma had made weekly visits to a lavish hotel that was owned by an old friend of his papa's. A friend who claimed to have no idea what business brought Cesare Marinetti and his young secretary to Milan so often.

His father certainly incited loyalty in his friends and employees!

"Cesare was supposed to be in recovery by now," his aunt said as the dinner hour in the hospital came around and the smells of overcooked food filled the room. "Why is it taking them so long?"

"I wish I knew."

Unease curdled in his gut. Something must have gone wrong. Stefano knew it couldn't be good when the doctor strode into the waiting room an hour later, his scrubs damp with sweat, his expression a mask of concern.

"Signor Marinetti?" he asked.

"Here," he said and rose. "How is my father?"

The doctor motioned to a door. "Please. Let's go in here where we can talk in private."

Stefano took his aunt's arm and guided her into the private room. He'd faced many situations where he had to keep a cool head, but he'd never felt this nervous.

The surgeon didn't mince words. "The heart surgery went well. But as we were closing the graft site on his leg, your father suffered *colpo apoplettico*."

His aunt let out a keening sound that mirrored Stefano's fear for his father's recovery. The doctor's grave expression told Stefano the stroke was severe.

"How is he now?" Stefano asked.

The doctor's lips thinned a fraction, and Stefano guessed the man was trying to soften the blow. "Unconscious. We have stabilized him, but we have no idea of the damage done until he wakes up."

If he woke from the coma. The back of Stefano's throat went dry at the thought.

Time. His father needed time to heal before they could begin to think of any treatment.

"When can we see him?" Stefano asked.

"As soon as he's stable and moved into intensive care. Get some rest." The doctor left without another word, closing the door behind him to afford them continued privacy.

Stefano paced the smaller room, his emotions on the razor's edge. He'd never felt as sad and alone as he did now.

"I'm not leaving the hospital tonight, but I'll have my driver return you to your hotel."

"You will call me if you need me?" his aunt asked.

"Yes, of course."

This complication made Stefano more aware of his own morbidity.

He was bombarded with dire predictions.

His papa could die.

As he'd suspected all along, his papa wouldn't return to his post at Marinetti anytime soon. His papa's shipyard was in his sole control, along with all the promises and problems he'd run from all his life.

If it was any other failing business he'd acquired, he'd liquidate it immediately. But many of the men in his father's employ had worked there all their lives. Their chance for finding another job would not be easy.

Stefano was ruthless in business. But he wasn't heartless. He couldn't toss good men out onto the street.

Everyone at Marinetti was his responsibility now.

And Gemma. He needed her help more than ever. How the hell did she fit into his papa's life? How would she fit into his?

Time would tell.

Stefano settled into a chair that would surely give him a backache by dawn and placed a call to the yacht. "Have it brought in to port in the morning but do not let Miss Cardone leave."

He and Gemma must talk.

He had to know why she and his father had gone to Milan. He must know just what her role was in his papa's life before he could think of where she belonged in his.

Early the next morning, Gemma stood outside Cesare's room and watched him through the observation glass in the intensive care unit. Her nerves twitched with each *bleep*, *whoosh* and *click* of the intensive care machines. Her heart broke to see the strong man lying so still, his gaze trained toward the ceiling.

She longed to sit beside him for a while and just talk like they had countless times. But nobody was allowed in his room.

Nobody but family and they weren't around.

"May I help you?" a nurse said, startling her.

"Where is his family?" she asked, annoyed that Stefano wasn't here by his father's side.

"His son and sister just left a few minutes ago," the nurse said, and Gemma wondered if they had gone out for breakfast. Perhaps Stefano was en route to his ship to fetch her. Wouldn't he be surprised, and not in a good way?

"I expect they will return within the hour," the nurse said. "Are you a friend of the family?"

"I'm Cesare's personal secretary. How is he?"

"He suffered a stroke during surgery but he is stable now," the nurse said.

"His prognosis?"

The nurse shook her head and moved away, leaving Gemma to wonder if she was refusing to answer or if Cesare's condition was that dire. She feared it was the latter.

Mio Dio! Cesare had told her this was a possibility during the surgery he faced and she'd refused to believe it could happen to him.

Take care of Rachel, he'd told her.

That responsibility rested heavier on her now. How could she possibly see to the child's needs and be Stefano's willing mistress as well? How could she continue to keep the two worlds apart?

One month. That's all she had to abide by Stefano's agreement. Never mind that she'd felt whole and wanted and loved in his arms. Never mind that she hadn't wanted the moment to end.

Cesare was adamant that Stefano not know about Rachel. He didn't trust his own son with his love child's care. But could he have misjudged his son? Could she trust Stefano with the truth?

She wished she knew!

Her head spun just thinking of the needs Rachel still required. The private school and nanny were another matter. Had Cesare made arrangements for Rachel's future?

She hoped so for she couldn't turn Rachel down. Not after investing so much of herself in the child's recovery.

"I'll take care of Rachel," she whispered, wishing Cesare was awake and could hear her promise. *But it won't be easy*, she silently added.

How could she possibly manage it alone?

The scuff of a shoe behind her snapped her from her dire musings. Someone was very close to her, and the energy crackling in the air could only be generated from one arrogant Italian. *Stefano*.

Gemma steadied her breathing the best she could and turned, but her chest felt too tight and her stomach knotted with dread as her gaze clashed with Stefano Marinetti's flashing dark eyes.

He was the embodiment of a Roman sentry garbed in tailored Armani and a glacial scowl. Anger eddied off him in heat waves.

"A word in private with you," he said, his voice sharp and disapproving.

"Of course," Gemma said, not wishing to vent her anger in front of the nurses.

But she lifted her chin to let Stefano know she was not sorry she'd defied him. All show, for her insides quaked with uncertainty and fear. Not fear for herself.

No, for Cesare's recovery and for his child. For her

own agreement with Stefano. What would the future hold for them?

She pushed past the man she'd loved to distraction last night and came face-to-face with an older woman. Even if the family resemblance hadn't been unmistakable, Gemma knew this was Cesare's sister.

"*E' questa la donna?*" the woman asked Stefano, her dark eyes as censoring as her nephew's.

"*Sì,*" he said, leaving Gemma to wonder what he'd told his aunt about her.

Nothing good she was sure, given he bore no resemblance to the gentle, sensual man she'd made love with last night. And could that have been his goal all along? Had he set out to break down her defenses with the love she craved so she'd reveal his father's secrets?

Had he tried to seduce her into trusting him?

If so then he'd misjudged her loyalty to Cesare.

From what she'd learned of him, he disliked being wrong or bested. Right now hard, unyielding Stefano ruled in the light of day, and it was obvious he was furious with her for escaping his yacht and coming here.

So she hurried down the hall with his hand pressed to the small of her back. Thankfully nobody could hear her knees knock with worry.

Nobody but her felt her heart aching with indecision. That small, dominating hold on her was creating havoc within her, reminding her of the passion they'd shared. Of the heat that still flared between them.

Was that all it was? Sex?

It must be. But even as she settled on that reason, she feared that another emotion had begun to take root last night. Love.

Last night he'd made love to her so thoroughly and so

deeply that her heart had beat in tandem with his. She'd seen a tenderness in him that he kept hidden, a vulnerability that she'd glimpsed once before when he'd mentioned his sister-in-law's deceit.

She'd sensed his raw need tinged with fear and her heart had melted then and there. She'd ached to comfort him. To hold him into the night. To love him now and forever.

She'd melded with the soul of the man and knew he was capable of intense compassion as well as passion. She wanted to believe he'd embrace the role of Rachel's brother. She wanted to trust that Stefano Marinetti would finally put family above business and himself. She wanted to believe all would be right.

And now? Now in the harsh light of day the ruthless, arrogant Stefano was back in control. She slipped into the alcove and whirled on him, breaking the contact that muddled her mind so.

When it came to business, Stefano was brutal.

When it came to family, he'd walked away before without a care. She couldn't let that happen to Rachel. She couldn't let him hurt her, either.

He pressed Gemma against the wall and stood over her, his hard, lean body centimeters from hers. It was a pose she'd seen countless times between couples on the street when they wanted a private moment to share a few words.

Or to share a kiss.

A delicious shiver ran through her and she damned her body's eager response to his. Here and gone, leaving an intense ache of want. Leaving her trembling.

"You were to wait on the ship for me," he said in a furious whisper that raised bumps on her skin.

She'd not allow him to heap guilt on her. "I was worried about your papa, and you."

The pulse in his temple beat madly, belying the cocky

smile he affected. "He is unconscious, *bella*. The doctors don't know when he'll awaken or what condition he'll be in when and if he does."

Just what she'd feared. "I'm so sorry, Stefano. If there is anything I can do—"

"You can obey a direct order from now on, okay?"

"Of course," she said and hoped he couldn't hear the lie in her voice.

He shifted closer, his mouth quirking just so while desire softened the hard glint in his eyes. "What is going through your mind right now?"

Unbidden came the memory of them locked together in passion, writhing as one. She quivered at each deep rasp of his breath, of his spicy scent that teased her senses and clung to her skin yesterday morning. That seemed a lifetime away now.

He'd been dominant yet gentle, not this domineering man who had the ability to shift from intractable to sensual in the blink of an eye. Right now it was all she could do to keep her spine pressed to the wall when she wanted to bow into his body.

"I'm concerned about Cesare," she said. "And we have unsettled business between us."

"You are worried about our personal contract?"

She nodded, for though she wanted to trust him at his word, she knew she'd be a fool to do so. Especially since she was sure to displease him when she suddenly disappeared later today.

He lightly grazed her cheek with a bent knuckle. Tendrils of energy flowed from his touch to set her insides spiraling out of control.

"It will be drafted by tomorrow and ready for your signature," he breathed near her ear.

She gave in to a shiver. "Good. I can sign it when I return from visiting my nonna."

"When did you decide to do this?" he asked, trailing that finger down her throat.

"After that episode with my brother," she breathed, fighting the urge to tip her head back and sigh her pleasure.

"I'll go with you."

"No. I need to do this alone and you need to stay here with Cesare," she said, and when his eyes narrowed she added, "Please. She wouldn't understand me bringing my boss home."

"Very well. We will sign the papers upon your return, then celebrate tomorrow night, hmm?"

"Yes," she said, her breath quickening at the thought of lying in his arms again.

His fingers stroked her throat before spreading around her neck, not with threatening pressure but firm nonetheless. "Who is Rachel?"

She went deadly still, unable to move. He'd heard her talking to herself after all.

Gemma couldn't swallow. Couldn't do anything but stare up into his eyes that had gone hard and black again.

"The child of a dear friend," she said, speaking the truth and knowing he'd doubt her.

"Don't lie to me," he said.

"I'm not," she said.

She sensed the subtle shift of emotion in Stefano, a tightening of his muscles. A snap of annoyance in his eyes.

He pressed his face close to hers and she helplessly lifted her head for the kiss that wasn't about to come. And why would she even want to kiss a man who was being irrationally obdurate?

But he surprised her with a quick, hard kiss that left her

wanting so much more. He withdrew his mobile and punched in a number. "I'll have my driver take you to the train station. He'll be waiting for you at the door."

"That isn't necessary."

"I insist."

He was laying down an order that she had no intention of obeying.

She had something important to do before she boarded the train to Milan. Something that would only raise more questions if he knew. Questions that she still couldn't answer.

"Thank you," she said with a smile, and hoped to hell he couldn't read the lie in her eyes.

CHAPTER NINE

T<small>HE</small> second his driver phoned to let him know that Miss Cardone had never left the hospital, Stefano knew she'd tricked him. She'd looked him in the eyes as the lie tumbled from her ripe lips.

She must have slipped out a side door of the hospital. But as he stood outside under a full Tuscan sun, he had no way to know which direction she'd taken.

This was Saturday morning. Whether she'd visit her nonna in Manarolo was moot. If her habits held to form, she would take the train to Milan.

This time instead of traveling with his papa, she'd go alone. Unless Stefano was lucky enough to speed to the station and catch her before her train left.

He'd just about decided she'd caught the train that had just pulled out when he saw her hurry into the train station. She had a carry-on gripped in one hand and a wrapped package in the other. A gift. For the mysterious Rachel?

Though his possessive bent urged him to make his presence known now, he feared she'd likely forfeit her visit if he did so. Such loyalty to his papa!

What did he have to do to earn that same devotion?

Trust.

He'd never granted it to her, nor had she to him. They were very much like feral cats circling one another, both wary, both knowing any mating would come in an explosion of emotion.

Perhaps that was what drew him to her. She didn't throw herself at him or play mind games as too many of the women he'd dated had done.

With the exception of these jaunts she'd taken to Milan, she'd been honest and real with him. He was surprised that he enjoyed being with her more than he'd ever enjoyed the company of another woman. She held his interest and stoked his desire, whether they were verbally sparring or making love.

Yes, he'd used the wrong tactic with Gemma Cardone from the start. She didn't cower to threats or confess all in the throes of passion. She kept her head and she held her confidences close to the heart.

Too close perhaps, for she put her loyalty above all else.

Milan.

The city she and his father had escaped to with aching regularity. He suspected that he'd find the mysterious Rachel here.

The child of a friend.

What he couldn't imagine was how the hell had his father figured into this?

A grim smile touched his lips as the train chugged toward Milan. It was just a matter of time now before he caught her in her lies.

The trill of her phone sounded overly loud in the confines of the train. Gemma answered it immediately, fearing that Cesare had taken a turn for the worse and Stefano was calling her.

Instead it was the banker she'd contacted a couple of days ago regarding the loan. Before she could tell him it wasn't necessary, he launched into a heated diatribe of the shortcomings of the inn.

"Our inspectors paid special care to the property," he began, "and there wasn't any evidence that restorations had been done in years."

"That's impossible. I sent home thousands of euros for the repairs."

"Perhaps you did," the banker said. "But I can assure you not a bit of it was used to upgrade or repair the inn. For that reason alone we can't possibly grant a loan for any amount."

She hung up, dazed and heartsick. She didn't doubt the man. Nor did she have to wonder what had happened.

She'd trusted her brother to see to the renovations. She'd believed him when he'd given her updates. She'd been grateful that she hadn't had to take time away from her initial healing, and then from her job to see to the work herself.

He and his wife had lied to her for a year. She doubted Nonna was aware of it, for she'd only promised she'd make the inn a beautiful place again.

No wonder the older woman had given Emilio her shares. He'd clearly deceived her as well.

And the money? He'd gambled it away. She was sure of it.

Her heart ached for what she must do now. She had to tell Stefano the truth.

She couldn't deceive him in this since he'd paid her brother a fat sum for his shares. It didn't matter that he was rich and could afford the loss.

She couldn't welcome him into her arms with another lie between them. If he discovered the state of the inn, he'd surely believe she'd duped him from the start.

No, she'd have to trust he'd believe her in this. And if he didn't?

Gemma swallowed hard and stared out the window. If he rescinded his offer, fired her or both, she didn't know what she'd do.

Stefano wondered who'd phoned Gemma for though the call was brief, it had changed her demeanor. Perhaps deflated her spirits was a more accurate description.

Her smile had vanished and she appeared pensive.

He ached to go to her. Comfort her. But he couldn't let her know he was following her for she'd likely alter her plans.

He couldn't risk that, not after coming this far, not when he would finally discover who Rachel was and what her tie was between Gemma and his father.

So he shifted uneasily on the bench and tried to harden his heart to her distress. For the first time he failed miserably.

The Benevenuto Scuola sprawled on the fringe of the second ancient wall surrounding Milan and provided a relatively large yard for exercise in a city that was mostly marble and concrete. Like the private school Stefano had attended as a boy, the building was aged.

But old in Milan screamed Renaissance and this school was no exception.

He'd kept a careful distance from Gemma as she wound her way from the train station to the school. But now that she was going inside, he picked up his pace.

He didn't wish to lose her after trailing her across Italy. The sun had warmed his body while the rumba sway of her hips had heated his blood.

The spirited *clack* of her heels on the marble floor echoed in the vast hall like a pagan beat. He felt her tension pound in his head, felt her anxiety reach out to him, felt her pulse thrum in time with his own.

She was a few feet from a massive horseshoe staircase that rose to a second floor. Students milled about on the balcony with some leaning over the thick marble banister.

They were all adolescent girls dressed in sedate uniforms, and he'd place the pupils in age from six to mid-teens.

"Gemma!" One girl's shout echoed over the hum of voices.

Stefano picked up his pace and closed the distance between him and Gemma. Not that he had to rush now.

A young girl raced down the staircase and threw herself into Gemma's waiting arms. The two erupted in laughter and girlish giggles: She must be Rachel.

"Look at you," Gemma said, holding the girl away from her. "You've grown another inch since I last saw you."

The girl beamed and his insides twisted. No! His eyes must be deceiving him.

He rocked to a stop a few feet behind the pair, thunder-struck by the girl's unmistakable family resemblance. She was a Marinetti. He was certain of it. But who was her father?

The girl noticed him then and went just as still. But her shock lasted less than a second.

She tore herself from Gemma's arms and rushed to him, but seemed to barely restrain the impulse to launch herself into his arms. "You finally came!"

"No, Rachel," Gemma said, trying to catch the girl.

But it was too late.

Rachel stood before him, her smile wide and her eyes glittering with unmistakable joy as if challenging him to return the favor. "You are more handsome in real life than in your pictures."

"*Grazia*," he found himself saying, captivated by her exuberance. "You know who I am?"

She giggled at that. "Of course, I know! Papa brought me pictures so I'd know my half brother."

Maledizione! Rachel was his father's love child.

His mamma had been right. His father had engaged in an affair. But it hadn't been recent as she'd feared.

Rachel wasn't shy or reserved. No, she was boisterous and outrageous and clearly starving for attention.

"Rachel, please." Gemma pulled the girl back and put a meter or two between her and Stefano.

"Where is Papa?" Rachel asked, looking from him to Gemma. "Didn't he come, too?"

"Not this time," Gemma said, seeming pale and far too nervous. "But he sent you this."

Gemma gave the girl the package she'd carried from Viareggio.

Rachel tore into it and squealed. "He's a perfectly gorgeous kitten. Is it angora like the others?"

"Perhaps." Gemma's flush gave her away, but Rachel didn't seem to notice. But he did and he'd bet angora kitties didn't come cheap.

"Why don't you put your new kitty in your room and then we'll leave?" Gemma said.

"Okay. I'll be right back," Rachel said, then looked him square in the eyes. "Are you coming to the doctor with us?"

"No," Gemma said.

He allowed a smile that felt as tight as his nerves. "Of course I will."

Rachel beamed before racing off up the stairs, and the wall of reserve inside him shifted. Nobody had ever seemed that pleased to be in his company before.

"How dare you follow me," Gemma said, turning on him like a pit viper.

He cocked an eyebrow, torn between amusement and rage over her part in this deception. "Why wasn't I told I had a *sorellastra*?"

"Ask Cesare," she said.

"Are you saying you don't know?" He loosed a humorless laugh when he was tempted to curse the walls down because she was still refusing to be honest with him. "You are his private secretary. You know all of his business, all of his dirty secrets so I am sure you know why the hell my father chose to keep his love child a secret."

She cupped her hands to her face and trembled. "Look around you, Stefano. This isn't the place to discuss this."

He set his teeth, hating that she was right, hating it more that he'd lost control of his emotions in public, no less. That had never happened before he'd met Gemma Cardone. Now he was changing before his own eyes into a man he scarcely knew.

"Is she the only one or did my father have others he kept apart from us?" he asked.

"As far as I know Rachel is his only illegitimate child."

And that half sister was rushing back down the stairs with a smile that rivaled the sun.

"Where is her mother?" he asked.

"We don't know," she said, and the tense line of her shoulders drooped even more. "She abandoned Rachel at the hospital when she was six years old."

Not a sterling character endorsement for his father's lover. "Her age now?"

"Seven."

That was when Stefano had graduated from the university and began working at Marinetti. He'd brimmed with new ideas to improve the company—ideas his father had refused to consider.

Cesare had wanted Marinetti to remain the solid old company that his father and his father before him had managed. "Marinetti Shipyard prides itself on tradition," his father had said, and of course Davide had agreed. "We are loyal to the community, our employees and our customers."

And all the while his father had been forcing Stefano to stand on old-world standards, he had been having an affair.

Gemma could not quell the trembling inside her. Stefano sat on the other side of Rachel in the oncologist's office and remained calm. Too calm, in her opinion.

He had to wonder about the state of Rachel's health. He had to notice that his chatty half sister had gone unnaturally quiet.

But he didn't ask questions and he didn't attempt to make small talk. He just sat beside his half sister and skimmed through a magazine.

On money, no less!

The inner office door opened and a nurse offered a benign smile. "Rachel Pantaleone."

Gemma rose with Rachel and wondered if the girl's name struck a chord in Stefano. Something surely had prompted that black scowl again.

"Do you want me to accompany you?" he asked Rachel, flooring Gemma by asking that.

"Yes, please," Rachel said and took his hand just like she always had done with her father.

Tears instantly stung Gemma's eyes for deep down she'd prayed that Cesare would confide in his family one day. She'd hoped that he'd welcome Rachel into his home instead of leaving her here in this elite school apart from her family.

Of course the girl would gravitate to Stefano. He oozed confidence. Plus he was more than six feet of sensual sophistication, broad-shouldered and heart-poundingly handsome.

But she'd never dreamed that Stefano would be so patient and attentive to his sister.

Of course she knew he was determined to unearth all of his father's secrets regarding Rachel. That would surely test the heart of this man when he learned of Gemma's involvement.

The doctor entered with a smile. "I see you have brought someone new along."

Rachel giggled. "This is my brother, Stefano. He's very rich and very handsome."

"Rachel," Gemma scolded in hopes of saving the doctor embarrassment.

"Don't you think he's handsome?" Rachel asked her.

Gemma knew her face was flame-red. "Yes, very handsome," she repeated and hoped that would be the end of it.

The doctor thankfully stepped in and extended her hand to Stefano. "I am Dr. La Rizza, by the way."

"My pleasure," Stefano said.

"I read an article about your latest eco-friendly yacht," she said. "Very impressive."

"I can give you a tour if you are interested." He paused a beat and flashed the doctor a smile. "Or if you are just curious and would like a day away from these walls, you have only to ask."

Gemma went tense and edgy again, and this time she was certain of the cause. Jealousy. Stefano looked at her with that same hunger when they made love.

Right now he acted as if he'd enjoy doing the same with the doctor. And his adolescent sister was sitting in the room!

An adolescent sister who clearly was enthralled by her

brother as well. But where Rachel was trusting the brother she'd only heard about, Gemma was more circumspect. As she'd discovered of late, brothers could deceive in the cruelest of ways.

If her own brother whom she'd loved and nurtured could stab her in the back, how safe could Rachel be with a sibling who was a virtual stranger? One who'd had no difficulty turning his back on his family before.

"I assume you are aware we are still keeping close watch over Rachel," the doctor said to Stefano.

Stefano made a seesaw motion with one long-fingered hand as if to indicate that he only had a sketchy idea of all Rachel had been through and what she still faced. "I would appreciate it if you would enlighten me."

"Gladly." The doctor launched into a detailed version of Rachel's surgery, recovery and regimen of drugs designed to hold her markers low.

"I don't want to guess what the outcome would've been if you hadn't found a donor," he said.

The doctor inclined her head. "We would not be here now."

"Papa was upset that he wasn't a match," Rachel said.

"I should hope so," Stefano said. "It would've grieved me to know I could not save my sister's life."

"Would you have donated your marrow?" Gemma asked.

"Without hesitation," he said, and she knew he meant it.

This was a side of him that she'd never seen before and she didn't know quite what to make of the changes. Gone was the austere demeanor. He seemed younger. More relaxed. More open.

"If you've no more questions, I'll return to talk with you after Rachel's CT scan and blood work is finished," the doctor said.

Gemma forced a calm mien as the nurse took Rachel from

the room for her tests. The old worry that the girl's numbers would be high or the technician would see something that indicated the cancer had returned plagued her.

She wanted her to be free of the disease that had taken her own mother's life. She'd failed to save her mother and this was her redemption. More, actually, for she'd come to know Rachel and love the child nobody had wanted.

The second the door to the examination room closed, the walls fairly swelled with tension. She turned to Stefano who was watching her with eyes that mirrored the depth and mystery of the Mediterranean Sea.

"Why wasn't I consulted as a bone marrow donor?" Stefano asked, pushing to his feet to prowl the small room.

Why indeed? Gemma could only guess from what Cesare had told her.

"Your father didn't want his wife to know about Rachel. If you'd been called in to test for a match, his secret would have been revealed," she said.

His hand cut the air in an impatient gesture she'd come to recognize. "Was he too cowardly to confess his infidelity?"

"Perhaps protective is a better word," Gemma said. "He told me his wife lacked a forgiving nature and she'd already suffered enough grief with the death of your brother and his family."

The grim lines on his face told her that he'd suffered as well. "He should have told her about his love child years ago."

She shook her head. "Cesare didn't know Rachel existed until a year ago. That's when a social worker at the hospital contacted him about her grave condition."

He scrubbed a hand over his mouth. "Was it before or after Davide's accident?"

"After," she said. "Rachel was sick. Dying. He'd just buried one son and family. He couldn't let his daughter die as well. So he took money from the company and from his wife's trust fund to pay for Rachel's care."

He cut her a cold look that enveloped her in ice, but she refused to shrink from his anger on this. For Rachel she'd brave anything—she had braved it already by facing her deepest fears.

"How in the hell did a woman from Manarolo become involved in my father's business? Was it money?"

The accusation stung, but considering the troubled past between them, she let the comment go.

Tell him all of it. Get it all out in the open now. But that meant she'd have to divulge her own fears and guilt.

"I attended university in Milan and volunteered at the hospital every weekend," she admitted. "I was working here nights when Rachel was admitted. There was a letter with her explaining that the mother could no longer care for her. Cesare was listed as the father, so we notified him."

"He took a paternity test?"

"Right away and it was conclusive proof."

"That is obvious just looking at her," he said. "I take it you were the stranger my papa could confide in."

"Yes." And the one whose marrow was a perfect match, but she couldn't bring herself to discuss that now, not when there was a greater issue at stake.

"Now that you know about Rachel, you can see that she leads a normal life. She shouldn't have to remain hidden here."

He stalked to the window and splayed a hand on the glass, the fingers long and bent just enough to remind her his relative calm was a tenuous thing—as if she needed a reminder!

"The school Rachel attends is elite but it is not a boarding school," he said. "Who takes care of her?"

"Your father hired a nanny who sees to Rachel's daily needs, but it isn't the same as living with family."

"Does Rachel know the difference?"

"I'm sure she does," Gemma said. "She needs to live in Viareggio with her family. She deserves to live a normal life."

"Normal how?" he asked. "I went to a private school. I rarely saw my family. This doesn't differ that much. The girl attends school in Milan. Her doctors are in Milan."

"In other words she is out of your hair if she stays here," she said, and when he didn't refute that she wanted to scream. "Of course you'd take this stance."

"It is logical and the best solution for my half sister."

Couldn't he address the child by name? "You've no idea what is best for Rachel. You don't know her and it is clear you have no intention of getting to know her."

A charged quiet arced between them, like the wake of an electrical storm. He didn't pace. He didn't scowl. He just stared at her with a face burned clean of emotions.

"My father arranged for her to stay here so I trust this was his choice," Stefano said.

He would take that logic. "It was his only choice at the time. Keeping Rachel here was ideal during the worst of her medical care, but of late Cesare had talked about moving her to Viareggio."

"That is out of the question now," he said. "My father's doctors say it is unlikely he will recover enough to care for himself, let alone a business and a child."

Gemma had suspected as much, but hearing it made her heart ache for Cesare and Rachel. She met Stefano's stoic gaze without flinching despite the stab of regret that he wouldn't open his arms and heart to Rachel.

"You should know that Cesare asked me to assume

Rachel's care should something happen to him, and I trust he made the proper arrangement," she said and hoped that were true. "You will not have to bother yourself about her welfare."

"Did my father establish a separate trust fund for her?" he asked. "Is that why you are so keen to take over the care of my sister? Do you hope to gain control of her fortune?"

The verbal slap sent her emotions reeling again. "I am doing this because I love her. If Cesare set aside any money for Rachel, it will be hers."

"How noble of you." He straightened, becoming six foot three of domineering male. "She is not your responsibility."

A chill whispered over Gemma's heart as she stared into his enigmatic eyes and read the challenge there. "You don't want her so why are you fighting me on this?"

"She is a Marinetti."

As if saying that meant anything. "She's a child in need of love. I can give her that. Can you?"

"I will provide for my sister."

She stamped a foot in frustration. "That is not the same thing as opening your heart to her!"

"I am her brother," he said. "If my father can no longer see to Rachel's care then it falls to me."

"You don't want her."

"I doubt my father did, either," he said.

Gemma moved to the other window and stared out at a city that bustled with activity for she simply couldn't bear to look into Stefano's hard eyes again.

Was there any way that she could reach his heart? Could she get him to see that having his family around him would make him a better man?

"You're wrong," she said. "Cesare could have stood by and done nothing to save Rachel, but he hired the best doctors. He sat by her bedside when she was frail and sickly and given little chance to survive even after they found a perfect donor match. Does that sound like a man who didn't want to be near his child?"

Stefano was silent for so long she feared he wouldn't answer her. "No, it does not."

She didn't delude herself into thinking that small concession was a sign he'd softened. She doubted that Stefano had ever conceded defeat in his life.

But she couldn't give up Rachel, either. "Please, let me assume her care. She needs me."

He turned her to face him and nudged her chin up with a curled finger, his touch igniting a torrent of conflicting emotions in her—anger, fear, desire.

"Does she really need you, *bella*? Or do you need her?"

CHAPTER TEN

THE lush lips that trembled apart confirmed what Stefano had sensed in her. Gemma Cardone was obsessed with seeing to his sister's welfare.

It made no sense to him that a stranger would become so attached to a sick child, especially one she'd only known a short time. But it was clear his sister was equally close to Gemma—the two shared a bond that was as strong as blood ties.

"This donor that was a perfect match. It was you," he said, certain he had pieced that much together now.

She met his stare head-on. "Yes."

Her admission allowed the rest to fall into order. The massive sums of money his father had routinely spent in Milan had been for Rachel's care. The small fortune Gemma had suddenly acquired had been her reward for her life-giving marrow.

"You were well paid," he said.

"I didn't ask for the money or want it."

"Yet you took it anyway."

"Cesare insisted," she said.

"Did he also insist that you become his personal secretary?"

She bit her lip, and that slight hesitation was blood to a shark. She was still hiding something from him. But what?

"I needed a job," she said.

"And he needed a confidant as well as a secretary to manage his secret and his business."

"Yes. He never meant to hurt his family," she said.

He nodded, believing that as well. His father had found himself in a precarious position with a sick, illegitimate child and a jealous wife who would never have accepted Rachel.

"Are you related to Rachel?"

She shook her head and he knew before she voiced the denial that she was telling the truth. "No. Why do you ask?"

"I am trying to determine why a young woman would give so much to a stranger, even for free, as you claim."

She looked away, clearly uncomfortable again. "It was the right thing to do."

"Come now. You should know by now that you can trust me with your secret." He stroked her cheek with a finger and had the satisfaction of watching color bloom in its wake. "Why were you even tested, *bella*?"

She shrugged, but the movement screamed of soul-deep tension. "I was on the donor list as a possible match."

"Why were you on the list?"

She gave a sharp shake of her head as if a part of her was reluctant to share the truth. "I wanted to be of help. I wanted to save a life."

"There's more to it than that. Tell me."

She tried to pull away from him but he closed in on her, maintaining his hold and edging her further into distress. He had her trapped and they both knew it.

"Why, Gemma? Why did you put your name on a bone marrow registry?"

She trembled, quaking silently and uncontrollably. But it was her eyes filling with moisture that made his gut clench.

He'd never been moved by a woman's tears before, but he was now and that scared the hell out of him.

"Because I'd promised myself that I'd not hesitate to save a life if I ever had the chance to do so again," she said.

Again? "What happened before that drove you to do this?"

She swallowed hard, her eyes so glassy with moisture he was sure she could see nothing but the past that tormented her. For once his impatience crumbled around him. Seeing her in such raw pain lashed his soul and he drew her into his arms, offering her comfort and taking the same from her nearness.

"It's all right," he said, wiping away the silent tears that streamed down her face and feeling closer to her now than he had when they'd made love.

She sniffled loudly and tried to compose herself. "My mother had leukemia and needed a bone marrow transplant," she said at last. "Nobody in the family was a match. Nobody but me."

"You donated your marrow to save your mother?"

"No. I was confused and afraid." She bit her lower lip so hard he feared she'd draw blood. "I was too young to understand it all. Mamma insisted I be spared the pain of it."

"She was protecting you."

Again the abrupt shake of her head. "Perhaps that was part of it. But I was terrified of the procedure, selfish and fearful that giving part of me would somehow make me more vulnerable to the disease that was killing Mamma. I put my feelings above her life. I believed that in all of Italy they'd find another donor." She swallowed hard. "But they didn't."

He didn't know what to say to that, so he simply pulled her into his arms. "How old were you?"

"Twelve." She lifted her eyes to his then and his gut clenched from the guilt she'd heaped on herself. "I could have saved her life if I'd acted sooner, if I'd realized how desperately she needed me. By the time I agreed to be a donor, she was too weak for the surgery. She died the next day."

"*Bella*." Stefano cradled her close and dropped kisses on her closed eyes that were still damp with tears. "You must let the past go."

And wouldn't he be wise to take his own advice as well? He couldn't continue to think every woman was a gold-digger, that they were out for money and position.

He couldn't continue to isolate himself from his family, especially now with a gravely ill father and a sister who'd need care. No, a family.

As if reading his thoughts, she said, "Please think about moving Rachel to Viareggio."

The door opened and Rachel bounded into the room, putting an end to that conversation. "May we go for ices now?"

"That's a fabulous idea," Gemma said, her voice still holding a tremor of sadness. "Stefano? Will you join us?"

"I wouldn't dream of letting two lovely ladies leave without me," he said, gaining a squeal from his sister and a deepening blush from Gemma.

Her affection toward his sister touched something deep inside him. Something that had lain hidden for years.

She was a good woman. She'd make a fine mother. A fabulous wife. But was he ready for such a commitment? Or was he seeing her as the one who'd make his life easier, and his nights far more interesting?

He wished to hell he knew, for Gemma deserved more than what his money could offer her. She deserved his love.

Gemma had expected Stefano to be stiff and withdrawn around Rachel, but he treated her as if he'd known her all his life. As if she was family that he cared about.

In fact, it had been the most delightful day that she'd spent in his company, with the exception of baring her own soul. But even then he'd held her with such tenderness that she'd finally done as he'd suggested and let go of some of the guilt that had gripped her for so long.

Now the question remained what would the future hold for all of them. Gemma expected Stefano would be eager to return to Viareggio, but after seeing Rachel returned to her nanny at the modest house in Milan, he seemed in no hurry to leave.

"I am ravenous," he said as he escorted Gemma into an upscale restaurant. "You must be as well."

"Maybe a little hungry."

He smiled, a flash of teeth made more white against his tanned olive skin. The glint in his dark, magnetic eyes hinted he was hungry for more than food, but it was the slow curl of his fingers against the small of her back that had her own desire blossoming.

She swallowed hard and tried to concentrate on their surroundings, but a glance at the intimate tables and couples with eyes for each other only brought images of her and Stefano doing the same. How easy it would be to fall in love with him. Or had she already done that?

The waiter showed them to a table tucked in a corner that was made more private by the gorgeous specimens of potted ferns. He waited until Stefano had seated Gemma before rattling off an impressive wine list.

"The night calls for champagne," Stefano said, and Gemma wondered what had suddenly put him in such a celebratory mood.

"Would you like to hear the menu now?" the waiter asked, and at Stefano's nod, he listed the house specials.

All were marvelous dishes, but Gemma couldn't do justice

to a meal, not the way her stomach was in knots over this emotional day followed by this new side of Stefano.

She hoped that meeting his sister had brought about the change in him. Would he give his sister's care more thought? Would he finally realize the importance of family and embrace it instead of shunning it?

Or was he simply of a mind to romance her tonight? Her body warmed at the thought, even though her mind rebelled. She had too much to consider. Too many worries.

"You are in a rare mood," Gemma said after the waiter took himself off.

Stefano shrugged off the comment as usual, and it occurred to her that he wasn't comfortable with praise. "I am always at peace once I've made a major decision."

"Does this means you have changed your mind regarding Rachel?" she asked.

"That is as it should be for now."

For now. She clung to those two words and hoped that he would concede soon. That he'd welcome Rachel into his life and his home.

"Then what is your major decision?"

"This business between you and me."

Her heart pounded too hard and too fast. He must mean he'd finalized the contract.

Thirty days of uninhibited sex for the title to the inn. An inn that was in serious need of repair. An inn that wasn't worth a fraction of the money Stefano had paid for it.

He poured them both champagne, his movements slow and sure. He'd taken his suit jacket off and rolled up the sleeves of his stark white shirt.

The contrast between dark and light had never seemed so intense as she watched his shirt pull taut over the dark olive hue of his forearms that seemed darker thanks to the dusting of crisp black hair.

Just thinking of the erotic brush of his limbs and chest against her bare body had her trembling with desire. Her mouth went dry and warmth expanded between her thighs.

Tell him! Get it out in the open so there are no more secrets. But she couldn't find the words. Or maybe she simply couldn't find the courage.

For once he learned he'd been duped, he might tear up her contract this time. He'd likely send her packing well before her thirty days were up.

He sipped his champagne, his eyes taking on a gleam that sent her blood racing. "It is up to you if you leave Marinetti." He leaned forward and captured her startled gaze with his, her mind numb with confusion and her body too relaxed from the champagne. "I need a personal assistant to accompany me for the foreseeable future. I need you, *bella*."

Three words she'd longed to hear. "What about the contract?"

"To hell with it! The inn is yours," he said, surprising her again. "What you've done for my sister doesn't even come close to what my family owes you."

"I told you I didn't expect payment for that."

He made a slashing motion with his hand, dismissing her words. "You are efficient and smart and beautiful and you have nothing to keep you from traveling with me on business. Of course, I will triple the salary you are earning now."

Always money with him. He was used to buying what he wanted when he wanted it. And wasn't that what he was trying to do with her? Buy her compliance?

It was a given they'd remain lovers, for how could she be in this man's company and not fall into bed with him? Would he come to love her in time?

Then there was the money he offered. Money she desperately needed to make the necessary repairs to the inn.

"Well, *caro*?" he asked and held up his flute. "Do we have reason to celebrate?"

She swallowed hard and knew that there would be no turning back if she agreed to his demands. Her gaze lifted to his and she quaked at the desire blazing in his eyes.

Her lover. Her love.

A smile trembled on her lips. "I accept."

His full mouth pulled into a sensuous smile. He clinked his glass to hers, the picture of a man who had just gotten what he wanted.

"To our new association," he said.

"To us," she said, and knew that there was no turning back now.

Stefano lounged in the back of the limo with Gemma cradled to his side. For the first time in ages he felt content.

He had no doubt that Gemma would do a fantastic job seeing to his personal needs—outside of bed as well as in it.

At this point in his life he needed someone he could trust to be there for him anytime of the day or night.

"Is that the harbor ahead?" she asked.

"*Sì*. I called ahead and had the yacht brought to port."

She smiled and snuggled closer to him. "I dreaded that drive back to Viareggio tonight."

"As did I," he said. "I would prefer returning in comfort."

He trailed a hand down the smooth length of her arm, marveling at the silken texture of her skin and the hint of floral scent that teased his senses.

The tremor that streaked through her stroked his desire up another notch. He couldn't get her into bed soon enough!

Yet the ride from the dock to his yacht seemed endless. The cool breeze from the water failed to refresh him, either.

He wanted Gemma. Now that she'd agreed to be his assistant, he couldn't think of anything else but satisfying this raw hunger she awakened in him.

The walk from the mini harbor of his yacht to his stateroom seemed miles away tonight. Her light floral scent drifted in the passageway while the quick clip of her steps on marble sent blood pounding in his veins.

He pushed into his stateroom lit only by the muted accent lights. It was enough to see by and complemented the sultry beat humming through his blood.

"*Bella*," he said, turning her in his arms and kissing her.

She welcomed him with open arms and sultry kisses, her tongue dueling with his in perfect tandem while her body moved against his with just enough hesitation to stroke his ego.

He gladly would lead in this for he knew what would give them both supreme pleasure. What stunned him was this odd sense that this was all new for him as well.

A novelty? He didn't know.

Right now he didn't give a damn about whys and hows. Her small hands did a slow crawl up his arms to send a new firestorm of need coursing through him.

He fumbled with the fastening of her clothes, something that he usually dealt with, with ease. But this task was made more challenging because he could not bear to take his mouth from hers. He didn't want to be parted from her for a second.

She tasted of champagne and sizzling desire. Her body writhed against his in silent demand and he was eager to comply.

She responded so genuinely to each stroke, each kiss, that his own head pulsed with the promise of intense pleasure. Yet the clothes that still clung to her deprived him of exploring her at his leisure.

He set her away and began to strip her to the skin, hating the restriction of his clothes as well, hating to forestall the inevitable. "You drive me wild with desire."

She smiled a siren's smile and flicked the clasp at her shoulder, releasing the slinky dress without effort. It glided down her body to pool at her feet.

His breath caught as golden light kissed the upper swells of her breasts, caressed her rounded hips and skimmed the dusky hair between her thighs.

"You are beautiful," he said.

"So are you," she said and his ego swelled along with his obvious desire for her.

And why wouldn't he when she stared at him with blatant appreciation? His skin felt too tight and his blood too hot to draw a decent breath, for she didn't posture and preen. She did nothing but stand before him beautifully naked while her gaze boldly caressed every inch of him.

It was another first for him, for the majority of his lovers had been intent on showing off their charms. Not so for Gemma.

She was as perfectly sculpted as the goddess of love. There was no artifice or trickery in her. Why hadn't he seen it before?

Because his mamma had believed her husband was being unfaithful and he'd not looked beyond that. He'd accepted her word that her marriage was failing.

Her demand for vengeance had nearly cost him the only woman he'd ever loved. *Loved*?

It couldn't be love, yet what else explained his obsession with her? The blinding jealousy when he thought of her lying in another man's arms. The sense of wholeness that encompassed him when he sank into her welcoming heat.

She was his lover—only his!—and she'd be his for as long as he wished. She'd been loyal to a fault with his father, holding the secrets he'd begged her to keep.

Stefano wanted that loyalty himself. He wanted Gemma to be his assistant, his confident, his lover.

Marriage?

He pushed that thought aside. He was not ready to commit to that yet. No, he needed to be sure that her affections were genuine. That she'd come to him because she couldn't bear to be apart from him, either.

That her claim to want him for himself and not his money wasn't a lie.

"*Mio amante*," he said, savoring the silken glide of her skin beneath his lips as he trailed kisses down the slender column of her throat. "*Mio amore*."

The seductive sigh that whispered from her swelled his ego and his groin. "I love you."

His body jolted, his heart skipping a beat at her avowal of love. He'd had lovers say them before. But he'd never *heard* the truth in them until now. He'd never believed there was such power in three words until they tumbled from Gemma's lush lips.

Of course she'd expect the same from him.

He loved her body. Loved her courage. Loved her loyalty. But as for this profession of his heart?

Stefano couldn't voice the lie. He wouldn't deceive her in this. He'd learned the hard way to guard his heart.

"This is just the beginning," he breathed before he sank into her and made them one.

She responded with sweet passion, her fingernails marking his back as her muscles clutched at him. There was no greed or artifice in her lovemaking, either.

She gave fully and he returned the passion with more tenderness than he'd known himself capable of.

Completion.

That was how it felt being with her.

It was a sensation that he looked forward to enjoying often. But he didn't delude himself into thinking it would last.

That would be a rarity.

That would mean he'd finally found the woman for him.

That would mean he could trust her fully and forever.

If he couldn't do that, then this passionate interlude with Gemma was just that. A stolen moment in time.

CHAPTER ELEVEN

GEMMA lay snuggled against Stefano's side, sated by his passion for now and lulled by the steady beat of his heart. She'd never thought to experience this deep emotional attachment to a man, especially so soon after meeting him.

To think that a short week ago she'd thought the very worst of him. She had thought him cold and calculating and callous. She'd thought him incapable of any tender emotions.

Now she was certain that he hid those softer traits from the world. Just the stroke of his finger brought her to extreme pleasure or tears of joy.

She wasn't one to cry—she'd cried out her tears long ago when her mother had been dying and she had blamed herself for not coming forward sooner. She'd vowed she'd give of herself again if she was fortunate to have the opportunity to save a life.

When that moment came, she hadn't hesitated going through the tests and the procedure for a stranger. She'd do it again if she could.

But though her heart had gone out to those in need, she'd never given so emotionally until she found herself in Stefano's arms.

She'd never known love until now.

He shifted, and just that slight brush of skin on skin was a seductive caress that stroked her desire awake again. It seemed unreal that she wanted more of what they'd shared not once but four times tonight.

It stunned her that she'd totally lost her heart to Stefano Marinetti. They were worlds apart, yet they'd found a common ground. Or was it just passion that bound them together?

She didn't like hearing that voice of doubt in her head. No man could make love to her with such tenderness and compassion if his heart wasn't involved.

And what about the job he had created just for her?

Hadn't he done that so they could spend the bulk of their time together? Wasn't that a clear sign that he wanted her to be a big part of his life?

As his mistress, not as his wife.

She grimaced at that, for she feared it hit too closely to the truth she didn't want to face.

Personal assistant had a far more respectable ring to it than paid consort.

Besides, if Stefano only wanted her as his mistress, he'd have said so. He wouldn't have created a mock position for her within his company.

No, the job was as real as the man. This was a sign he trusted her to manage his personal affairs. That had to include his family. And if it didn't? If she was just seeing what she wanted to see?

"What brought this troubled frown to your face?" he asked, placing a kiss on one eye and then another in a gesture so tender it brought tears to her eyes.

"I was thinking about family."

"There is not room for family in our bed, *caro*," he said, the nip he gave her chin releasing a deeper need in her.

She lifted her face to protest this sensual assault that was muddling her thoughts. Their lips clung in one long, delicious kiss that blotted everything from her mind but him. It was so easy to fall into his arms and forget the world.

But she fought against the drugging effects of his desire and pulled from him. "We need to talk, Stefano."

He grumbled and rolled onto his back, tossing one arm across his eyes. "Talk is the last thing I wish to do now."

Yes, one glance at his beautifully aroused body told her what he wanted—what he needed from her. "I hope that you will realize Rachel should live with you."

His muscular body tensed. Even the air seemed more charged than before as unease pinged over her bare skin to mock her nakedness. She'd bared all to him, even her soul. Yet he'd still held a part back from her.

"We have been over this before, *bella,*" he said. "If my father had wanted the world to know about Rachel he would have exposed her long ago. Instead he kept her tucked away in Milan where she is safe from a world she is ill-equipped to cope with."

She pulled the sheet around her, chilled by his refusal to consider a change of plans. "At first, yes, when her condition was so fragile. But Cesare did have a change of heart!"

She knew the moment the words popped out that there was no going back. The tension she'd sensed in him throbbed between them.

He sat up in one fluid motion. Though he looked semirelaxed, she knew that he could pounce on her in the blink of an eye.

"When?" he asked in that low, dangerous tone that skimmed along her nerves to leave her chilled.

For all the deep intimacies they'd just shared, she felt as if her soul was exposed. The fear of revealing everything only to incur his fury tempted her to lie, but there had been too many lies and half-truths between them already.

"The last Saturday we visited Rachel, Cesare told me that he wanted to bring her home," she said, beginning slowly so she could emotionally feel her way thorough this confession.

"To Viareggio."

If it were that simple… "To his house."

"Mamma would never have allowed that to happen!"

"Few women would welcome their husband's love child," she said. "But he was determined to make her see reason."

She dreaded to imagine the bitter words that had been volleyed between Cesare and his wife when he'd confessed his infidelity and then declared that he'd fathered a daughter that he wished to ensconce in their home. No wonder he'd suffered a heart attack!

"It is beyond the scope of reason why he would ask such a thing of my mother."

"Family," she said, stating the obvious. "He wanted his children united. He wanted his family whole."

"A wasted effort," Stefano said. "Mamma wasn't the for-giving sort."

"Like you?"

"Yes, like me."

"Then why are you insisting on managing Rachel's care when Cesare entrusted her to me?"

He whirled on her then, eyes snapping anger and some-thing that bordered on vulnerability. "She is a Marinetti."

She threw her hands in the air, having come full circle in this argument with him. "You assert that she's family yet you don't want her in your life. That isn't fair to her, Stefano, and it isn't what Cesare wants."

He snorted and sat up, his long legs dangling over the edge of the bed and his broad, muscular back racked with tension.

Every tender touch, each kiss, seemed as if it happened a lifetime ago instead of mere minutes.

"It is clear that my father spared no expense to hire a *bambinaia* and provide a safe home for my sister," he said. "So why the change of heart? When did he come to this decision to insert Rachel into his home?"

"He spoke of it often after Rachel's last visit to the doctor." In fact Cesare had been obsessed with the idea of having his daughter near him.

Stefano crossed to the window and peered out, and the setting sun poured through the window to dust his muscular frame in rose-gold. Her heart seized at the sight, for not one statue of a god in all of Italy could compare to his potent masculinity and rugged male beauty.

"Every time you and Papa went to Milan, my mamma would call me and complain bitterly of his infidelity."

"Why didn't she confront him?" she asked.

One bronzed shoulder lifted in a shrug. "An affair or two is expected in a marriage."

"I wouldn't be tolerant of infidelity," she said, needled by the sudden sting of jealousy at the thought of sharing Stefano with another woman.

"Nor would I," he admitted, surprising her. "I am faithful to my lover and demand the same."

She slipped from the bed and crossed to him, refusing to think that this synergy she shared with him would come to an end. "I'd never betray you."

"*Bella.*" He brushed a finger over her lips that still trembled from his possession, lips that quivered from holding back the last truth that seemed too large and ugly to reveal. "It was for the best that Mamma never knew about Rachel."

She sucked in a ragged breath and met his slumberous

eyes, knowing that what she had to say would turn his eyes black with disapproval again. But she couldn't continue to keep secrets between them, not now.

"She did know." She expected an immediate reaction and she got it.

He grabbed her arms then pulled her so close that she breathed the same charged air as he. "I don't believe you. Mamma would have told me if she'd known about Rachel."

"I'm sure she would have if she'd had time," she said, and rested a hand over his heart. "Cesare told her everything."

He shook off her gesture of comfort and prowled the room with long, angry strides. "When?"

"He unburdened his soul to her in the car on the way to their favorite restaurant in Tuscany." She crossed her arms over herself when he simply stared holes in her naked body. "He said they fought bitterly, that she flew into a rage the likes of which he'd never seen before."

He slammed the flat of his hand against the wall. "How could he think she would not react violently to such news?"

She shook her head, certain that Cesare hadn't thought his confession through. But then he hadn't known that his health would suddenly fail him, either.

"That's when the blinding pain hit him and he lost control of the car." She met his furious gaze and hoped he'd one day understand this. "When he woke, he learned he'd suffered a heart attack."

"He phoned you," Stefano said, his voice flat and hard.

She nodded. "From the hospital. He told me everything and begged me to protect Rachel."

"As well as guard his secrets?"

"Yes. He was afraid you would react worse than his wife if you knew."

"It's no wonder he is not improving," Stefano said. "He is mired in deep guilt over her death."

She wrung her hands together, wanting to reach out to him, wanting to offer him comfort, but she knew he'd not take it. Not now when his emotions were scraped raw again.

"He'll never forgive himself for what happened," she said. "So you will have to."

"And I would do this because?"

"Because he's your father. Because only a selfish bastard could be that indifferent toward his family."

He frowned, a fierce drawing of his brows that signaled he was far from accepting the truth. "What if I am, *bella*?"

It was a question Stefano had asked himself many times the past ten years. There had been many occasions when his mamma had phoned him, begging him to return to Marinetti.

He'd ignored her pleas just as he had avoided her repeated attempts to get him married.

Stefano had no desire for a wife or children at this point in his life. Perhaps one day when this inner drive for success abated.

Women were like water in his hands. His affairs never lasted long, for they all wanted more from him than he was willing to give.

Which made this tête-à-tête with Gemma short-lived at best.

Already they were clashing over how he should live his life! But he was also looking forward to the explosion of passion when they made peace.

But how could he think of that now? Gemma was tied neatly up in his father's lies. Yes, she'd done so out of loyalty to Cesare and his sister. But they were still lies!

"I don't believe you are as self-centered as you imagine yourself to be," she said at last.

He merely offered a wan smile. "Think what you will. I always put business first."

She shook her head. "You returned to tend to your father's business while he is recovering."

"*Bella*, my father will never manage Marinetti again," he said.

"Yes, I realize that now, but when you first agreed to lend him a hand—"

He placed a finger over her mouth to shush her. "I am not the prodigal son welcomed back into the family fold. My father suffered a heart attack and knew the situation was dire. He knew he couldn't continue and perhaps didn't have the heart to try after Mamma's death. That's why he called me, for he knew if I ever returned I'd assume control of Marinetti Shipyard."

Her face leached of color, but there was a glint in her eyes that hinted of lofty hopes. "You still have the obligation of family. Your father. Your sister."

"Do not imbue me with your character traits," he said. "I would see that both are well cared for to the best of my ability, and if that means bringing my sister and her *bambinaia* into my father's house, then so be it. But I won't sacrifice my life to do so."

"I haven't sacrificed to see that my family was cared for," she said.

"Haven't you?"

The question hung between them like an icy sheet. "If I did make some concessions, it was expected of me to care for my nonna and my younger brother."

He glared at her, angry she wasn't seeing herself in the same martyr's light as he. "What will you give the next time your family needs you? An arm? Perhaps an eye or kidney?"

"Stop it! I didn't sell my bone marrow," she said.

"No, but the end result was the same."

She let out a weary sigh. "Please, don't just move Rachel into your house and feel you've done the right thing. Make her part of your life. You won't regret it."

He wasn't so sure. How the hell would a sister and a young one at that fit into his hectic life? She wouldn't.

In fact his bachelor life was ill-suited for an impressionable young lady. But Gemma didn't see that part of the problem.

She likely saw herself still having a hand in his sister's life, carrying on as his papa had bade her to do. It was a pattern she fell into too easily. She took other peoples' lives to heart at the expense of her own.

"When did you give up on yourself?" he asked her, and before she could reply, added, "Was it when you blamed herself for your mamma's death?"

"I've not given up," she said. "I have dreams and aspirations."

"Tell me."

"I want to see the inn prosper again."

He made a cutting motion with his hand. "That's business. I'm talking about your personal life. What do you want to have two years from now?"

Their eyes met, and he read the love in hers before she looked away. "My own family."

Just as he'd thought.

Stefano couldn't expect her to remain his mistress forever.

She deserved marriage. Family.

She could be the one.

It'd been years since he'd let anyone get close to him. Especially a lover.

Gemma wasn't like his sister-in-law.

She was sweet. Amorous. Generous to a fault.

His sister adored her. His papa trusted her.

Could Stefano do no less?

He crossed to the en suite bathroom and paused at the door, glancing back at her and feeling his body stir with hunger. "We make port within the hour. Care to join me in the shower?"

That brought color blooming in her cheeks again. "I'll pass in favor of a few more minutes' sleep."

He smiled at the cause of her weariness and proceeded to enjoy a hot shower alone. Perhaps that was for the best. He was moving quickly with Gemma, but then he saw no reason to dawdle.

The sooner he got her ensconced in his home, the sooner he could get down to managing the two businesses. He certainly had a surfeit of that to attend to today.

Yet as the hot water pounded the tension from his shoulders and back, he found himself dreaming of the night to come with Gemma snuggled in his arms.

No woman had ever captivated him so. He'd been wrong to force her to be his mistress. She deserved more than that and he would damn well see that she got it.

CHAPTER TWELVE

GEMMA stepped into the salon and froze at the sight of Stefano giving rapid-fire orders over the phone. He'd dressed for the office, and with the copy machine and facsimile machines spitting out pages and his computer screen lit up, it was clear he'd started work before the sun rose.

The precision-fitted lines of his Armani suit could have served as armor, for he looked unapproachable. Invincible.

It was like stepping back to that first day he had taken over Marinetti Shipyard. The change in him from her passionate lover of the night to this ruthless businessman was dramatic.

The mesmerizing eyes that had glowed with passion were hard and calculating. The mouth that had moved over her body with erotic abandon was pulled into a tense line. Instead of greeting her with a smile or word, he simply nodded.

She had no idea if he was negotiating a major deal or grappling fast to stave off a catastrophe. Or an emergency?

Her heart stuttered as the most obvious reason for his anxiety crossed her mind. His father's tenuous condition. *Mio Dio, please not that*!

"What's wrong?" she asked when he finally ended the call, fearing his father had taken a turn for the worse. "Is Cesare all right?"

"Papa's condition hasn't changed."

She breathed a bit easier but not for long. Stefano's austere mood left her wary.

Whatever business deal he was engaged in had his full attention. She certainly pitied his opponent for it was clear Stefano was out to win.

"When will we make port?" she asked as she helped herself to cappuccino.

"In thirty minutes."

That still gave her over an hour to visit her flat and collect her mail, something she hadn't been able to do in days. "Can you spare me this morning? I have some business I need to attend to."

"Take all the time you want." He held his coffee cup in a punishing grip and scanned a paper, seeming distracted and harried. "I won't be needing you as my assistant after all."

"Excuse me?" She set her cup down with a clatter though her insides shattered in a million pieces. "What are you talking about?"

"I have given our situation much thought and decided you are right," he said. "Rachel needs a solid home environment. Since you have a close rapport with her, it seems fitting that we make a suitable home life together."

Had he gone mad? They'd just spent another night in each other's arms. He'd been more relaxed and playful than she'd ever seen him before. And now...

Now he was someone she didn't know.

"You can't expect for us to conduct an affair with a child in the house," she said.

"Of course not. We'll be married."

Married? Just like that he'd decided they should marry?

"Please start from the beginning and tell me what the hell

is going on," she said, desperate to know how the man who had made such passionate love with her had come to such a cold, unemotional decision in the light of day.

He gave her a negligent shrug and got to his feet with masculine grace, his expression devoid of anger or passion. "Forgive me for not explaining better. I've decided we will marry, by the week's end if it can be arranged. As we speak, my attorney is finalizing the wording on a prenuptial agreement that he'll fax over for you to sign."

Her mouth had dropped open, and for the life of her she couldn't seem to close it. Of all the scenarios she'd imagined regarding a marriage proposal, she'd never dreamed she'd be offered this cold business arrangement.

And that's exactly what this was! A business arrangement.

There was no tenderness. No concern for her feelings. No mention of love. *Because his heart wasn't in this.*

Like everything Stefano Marinetti did, this was business. This had been thought out to serve his purposes. Not *theirs*.

"You can't seriously think that I'll agree to this *business* arrangement," she said.

He looked up at her then and his brow snapped into a dark frown of annoyance. "Why not? You have said this is what Rachel needs. It's not like you don't love me."

The assured arrogance in that remark got her blood boiling and not in a good way. "What of you? What are your feelings toward me?"

He gave an impatient shrug. "I enjoy you more than I've ever enjoyed another woman."

Enjoyed. Not loved. Not the words she'd longed to hear. Not even a profession of affection like he'd shown when he'd asked her to be his mistress.

Mio Dio! Had his sister-in-law's deceit and his brother's

betrayal scarred him for life? Or had she been so blinded by
her own desire and love for this man that she failed to see that
he was incapable of such feelings?

She didn't know, but she couldn't accept this fate. Not
even for Rachel. She'd given enough. And wasn't it Stefano
who'd just upbraided her for letting her family use her?

A fax machine hummed to life and began spitting out
pages. The prenuptial agreement, she assumed, as he snatched
the papers from the tray and gave them an exacting read.

He grunted his approval, fanned the pages on his desk and
laid a pen atop them. "You'll note that I've given you a
generous settlement up-front. Just sign it so we can move on
to the next step."

"And that would be?" she asked, making no move to even
glance at the marriage contract.

"Obtaining the marriage license. If I can move quickly
enough, we can hold the wedding in two weeks when I return."

"Stop!" she said, hating the panic that made her voice
tremble. "Just stop and look at me."

He rocked back in his chair and stared at her with undis-
guised impatience. "Okay, I am looking at you."

But was he seeing her? Did he have any idea that he was
ripping her heart out with this unemotional proposal?

"Do you honestly think I'll agree to this?" she asked.

"In my circle marriages are still often tied to business." His
eyes narrowed to dangerous slits. "You object to the contract?"

She tossed both hands in the air. "I object to the fact you
are showing absolutely no emotion to what should be the
most wonderful day of our lives."

"Ah, you want, as they say, hearts and flowers and profes-
sions of the heart."

"Only if you mean it," she said. "I want to know what is

in your heart, Stefano. I want you to ask me to marry you, not tell me that is what we're to do."

"What difference does that make?" he asked.

It was a good question. A week ago she would've accepted this as her due. But not anymore.

She wanted to be romanced. Loved. She couldn't imagine marrying a man who didn't feel the same toward her.

"The difference is me saying yes to your outrageous proposal, or holding out for true love and walking out the door."

His mouth stretched into a flat, disagreeable line. "Is that a threat?"

"It's a fact," she said. "I deserve more than this. You are suddenly playing a tyrant here and I've no idea why."

A muscle worked frantically along his lean jaw, but it was the only sign that her impassioned words registered with him. *Mio Dio*, did what they'd shared mean nothing to him?

"I had hoped to finalize these arrangements before I flew to London today," he said, surprising her with that news as well.

That angered her all over again that he'd expected her to be ready at a moment's notice. "Why didn't you tell me we were going to England?"

"I am going, not you." He pushed to his feet and rounded the desk. "I chose you as my wife, *bella*. Your job will be to provide this good home environment for my sister, as well as for any children we'll have."

His words were frozen daggers piercing her heart. He'd not mentioned a loving marriage. He hadn't given the slightest indication she'd be anything more than the mother to his children and companion to his sister.

That was because this wasn't a marriage. It was a business deal.

Yet she wanted to be his wife. She wanted to be the mother to his children. She wanted to love him till the day she died.

But not like this. Not a one-sided affair where she'd soon be forgotten. Where he'd take a mistress to dote on. Love.

"What made you think I'd agree to this? That I'd be content to let you decide on everything regarding our future?" she asked, choking back tears for she wasn't about to cry in front of him.

"It is what you want," he said. "It is all I have to give. You know that, *bella*. I'll never hurt you."

"You're hurting me now with this."

"The marriage will be real."

"Will it?" she asked. "Do you love me?"

Silence exploded in the room, rocking her to her very soul. She felt the frisson streak through her, marbling her like an eggshell that could shatter at any second.

"I care for you more than I've ever cared for another woman."

But that wasn't love.

She couldn't fault him for his honesty now. He'd never professed to love her.

What they'd shared was perfectly fine for lovers. But not for a marriage. Not *her* marriage.

A bell chimed to signal they had reached the port. This was the end. She saw it in the hard sheen of his eyes and the stiffening of his body. She heard it in the frantic hammering of her heart.

What she had to do now was going to hurt more than words could say, but she refused to be used so coldly. "No! I can't do this. I can't be the convenient wife."

She turned and walked across the salon, her legs trembling so badly she feared she'd fall. Only pride and the urge to run and never look back kept her upright.

"What about Rachel?" he asked.

She faltered at that, for she'd promised Cesare she'd care for her. But how could she stay under these circumstances?

"Cesare hired a nanny to see to her needs. I'm sure she'll be able to remain in your employ." If not, his money would easily secure another.

"If you walk out now, it is over between us," he said. "Do you understand me?"

Oh, she understood him all right. She understood that he'd just broken her heart in two.

She hurried up the stairs and waited for the men to ready a dinghy to row her to shore. Waited for Stefano to appear and stop her, to take her in his arms and tell her he loved her, that he wanted to marry her, that he couldn't live his life without her.

But he didn't show his face as she was helped into the dinghy. She didn't see him at all as the small craft took to sea and she was rowed toward the jetty.

But she heard the whir of his helicopter as it lifted off the pad. The blades created a washboard of waves that sent the dinghy bobbing and her insides quaking.

In moments he was gone, leaving her life with the same drama as he'd stormed into it.

With one exception.

This time he was taking her heart with him.

"You're an ass, you know," Jean Paul said before he swilled down his fourth martini, not that Stefano was counting his friend's or his own alcohol consumption! "She is a desirable woman. I am tempted to return to her quaint inn in Manarolo if only to seduce her."

"Be my guest," Stefano said, but the shattering of the stemmed glass in his hand ruined his cavalier response.

Jean Paul merely smiled and shifted his lazy pose on the

upper deck chaise. He had declared that he and Stefano needed a few days away from the hectic pace and the launch of his new superyacht seemed the perfect excuse to get away.

Unfortunately Stefano had yet to relax. For one, he hadn't expected his friend to continually steer the conversation back to one flaxen-haired beauty who was never far from Stefano's mind.

Four months had gone by without him seeing Gemma. Four months in which he was certain she'd call him for some reason that required his immediate attention. Four months of silence when he'd been certain he'd planted his seed in her belly that last night on his yacht.

She would have the decency to let him know. Except she hadn't phoned him. If Jean Paul could be believed, she was still a slender beauty with all her curves in just the right places.

Her silence infuriated him. He wanted to know how miserable she was stuck in Manarolo. He needed to know that she missed him dreadfully and that she was sorry as hell for turning down his offer of marriage.

He couldn't go there of course, nor would he phone her to assess her mood. So he'd done the next best thing. He'd prevailed on his friend to visit the inn for much needed R & R after crashing his Peugeot at Le Mans.

He had *not* expected Jean Paul to fall in love with Gemma!

Since she was Stefano's former lover, he couldn't fault her if she found favor with another man. But did it have to be his best friend?

"I regret that I didn't buy Cardone's shares of the inn for myself," Jean Paul said after the bartender replenished his empty martini glass.

Stefano set his teeth, well aware his friend was determined to bait him again. "You are a Formula 1 driver who thrives on speed and power. What the hell would you want with half ownership of an antiquated inn in Cinque Terre?"

Jean Paul let out a long, satisfied sigh and smiled. "You have to ask?"

"No."

He knew what his friend would want with the inn and the woman running it. It was the same fantasy that kept him awake night after night, only he had lurid memories of him and Gemma tangled in the throes of passion that made it all the more tormenting to his peace of mind.

Not that he was likely to forget her with his sister asking about Gemma at every visit. She'd badger him twice as much after he moved her to Viareggio next month.

For now those jaunts tormented him more than enough. They reminded him of Gemma and her insistence that he move Rachel into the Marinetti mansion. That family was something to be cherished. *Every damned thing* reminded him of Gemma!

She was everything he despised and everything he desired. She was his bane and his salvation.

There was no way to rectify the two opposites.

Which wasn't far from the truth. Between the launch of his new superyacht and seeing that his father's needs were met, he'd had little time for anything.

Stefano squinted toward the east where the faint haze of the rugged Ligurian coast was just barely discernible. He'd never given Cinque Terre much thought before he met Gemma. Now he couldn't get the five tiny lands and one enticing woman out of his mind.

Jean Paul swung his feet over the edge of his chaise and sat up, staring at Stefano with cool blue eyes that were far too perceptive. "You must know that Gemma is nothing like your sister-in-law."

"I know, but I can't abide deceit."

Jean Paul frowned. "Apparently she can't, either. She was protecting her family, too, or at least trying to."

"That changes nothing."

He'd gone over it countless times and his anger still flared out of control when he thought how her family had used her. They'd still be using her if he hadn't interfered.

"You haven't forgiven her then?"

"No."

There was a long beat of silence that scraped over his nerves. "You are an ass," Jean Paul repeated, having come full circle in their conversation yet again.

Like she had done every morning since she'd returned to Manarolo, Gemma stepped out onto the balcony of her inn. At this hour before dawn, the lights from the settlement spilled over the fishing boats pulled to shore and spread out onto the tranquil bay in splotches of yellow and green.

There was nothing quite to compare with the beauty of a village coming awake. The night fishermen were just coming ashore while others that made their living by the light of day ambled down the winding lanes and steps toward their boats. Sounds of activity in the market intruded on the hush of morning as dawn slowly welcomed the new day.

The artificial lights of the night would fade as the sun rose, like a heavy wash on a watercolor painting. Her gaze swept over the village with a tumble of houses painted in salmon, dusty blue and old gold.

They clung to the deep crevice above the tiny cove as they had for generations. It was these moments where time seemed to stand still. It was then old memories returned and that she allowed herself to cry.

She could imagine that one of the fishing boats was her papa heading out to begin his day's work. Whenever a yacht dropped anchor near Manarolo for the night, her heart would race with anticipation that Stefano had finally decided to visit her.

She missed him dreadfully.

She missed all those she'd held close to her heart. Mamma and Papa had their lives taken from them too soon. Emilio and his wife had left Italy and she hadn't heard from them in months.

Dear Cesare had cheated death and, according to Rachel, was learning to walk again. The young girl phoned her weekly to update her with news about her papa, herself and Stefano. Always Stefano, who according to Rachel was far too busy with his businesses to enjoy life.

Up until one month ago Gemma had continued her weekly visits to Milan to see Rachel, too, being careful to go well before Stefano arrived.

But she would be denied that for Stefano had decided to remove his half sister to the Marinetti mansion in Viareggio. Wonderful news for Rachel, but it was just another person she'd loved who'd been removed from her life.

Gemma wiped the tears from her cheeks and lifted her face to the rising sun. The rattle of pots and pans echoing from the kitchen far below was a sign that Nonna was up as well.

The routine rarely changed. Even at times like now when they didn't have a boarder, her grandmother busied herself in a kitchen that was woefully outdated.

If only her brother had used the money Gemma had sent Nonna for the much needed restoration of the inn. If only she'd realized that giving him that much money was a powerful temptation to try his luck at the big casinos.

Gemma shook her head, saddened that she hadn't opened her eyes to the truth long ago. Stefano had been right—her brother had to learn to sink or swim. She couldn't continue to support him and his addiction.

Gold and pink bands of sunlight kissed the rooftops and stretched into the water, pushing back the last remnants of night. The azure sea glistened like a mirror, the tranquil expanse broken by the occasional fishing boat and the presence of one very large ship.

Her heart raced as she squinted at the superyacht anchored offshore. "Don't get your hopes up," she chided herself.

It was likely just one of the wealthy that came to play in the Mediterranean. Or perhaps it was Jean Paul who'd promised to return once his new yacht was completed.

She liked him, but she couldn't tolerate another visit where he outrageously flirted with her while extolling Stefano's virtues.

Stefano. If she could just get him from her mind.

Gemma tightened her shawl and headed downstairs. The restless energy pulsing inside her was driving her crazy.

In Viareggio she'd taken a long walk to work every morning. That habit was too ingrained to give up now.

She stepped from the inn and walked down the twisting lanes of the village to the main path to Riomaggiore. The entire walk took twenty minutes, but most days Gemma worked off the bulk of her excess energy midway.

Not so for today. Even with the sea crashing onto the cliffs at her right and the tidy vineyards and fragrant herbs growing profusely up the mountain on her left, her thoughts kept straying back to that huge yacht anchored offshore.

How long would she pine for Stefano? When would this intense longing leave her?

She reached the outcropping much sooner than usual, but she was still too keyed-up to stop and rest. But the second she stepped into the tiny cleared niche she came to a dead stop.

Gemma blinked but he was still there standing tall and un-yielding and oh so handsome. "Stefano?"

"You're early, *bella*."

For a heartbeat she couldn't breathe. How would he know that?

Jean Paul, of course. He'd been privy to Gemma's morning walks to clear her mind. He would've told his good friend about her odd schedule.

But why he'd kept Stefano updated didn't matter. A greater question begged to be asked.

"What are you doing in Manarolo?" *On Via dell'Amore*?

His smile came slowly, warming her more than the rising sun. "Waiting for you."

She absorbed that admission slowly and tried like hell not to read anything personal into it. Why was he waiting for her on the lover's walk instead of the inn?

She met his gaze and her mouth went dry. He looked at her with an intensity that made her knees go weak. His dark, sultry eyes caressed her and promised more.

And God, she ached to fall into his arms. But she wouldn't play the part of his convenient lover. She wasn't about to let any man use her—even though she couldn't imagine living without him. Even though she loved him with all her heart. Even though saying no to his cold proposal of marriage had been the most difficult thing she'd ever done.

Just being this close to him now was wreaking havoc on her emotions. She couldn't put herself through the pain of hoping for more from him than her occasional lover.

"Enjoy your stay on Manarolo," she said, and set off toward the path that wound to Riomaggiore with as much dignity as she could.

He stepped in front of her and grabbed her arms. "*Bella*."

Heat and longing exploded in her and she struggled to keep from leaning into his strength, into the promise sizzling in his eyes. *Mio Dio*, rejecting this man was nearly impossible to do when she longed to wrap her arms around him and hold on for dear life. But she couldn't go back. She couldn't be hurt again for the next time she may never recover.

"Don't," she said, brushing off his hold and then instantly mourning the loss.

She didn't have long to grieve.

He crowded her against the railing and slid his hands up her arms. Heat flares snapped the air in their wake as he bunched her shawl to her upper arms and made her burn for him, made her remember how very good they were together. Cool morning air whispered over her backside while an inferno of sensual masculinity blasted her from head to toe.

"Don't what?" he asked, his voice pitched to a velvet purr. "Don't touch you? Kiss you? Desire you?"

The last two words ribboned around her and held her fast to him, an invisible thread of need that couldn't be broken. *Don't hurt me*, she almost said. But that would be a waste of breath. Just standing in the shadow of his power was tearing her apart inside.

"Why are you here?" she asked again, hugging her shawl around her when what she really wanted was to press her palms against his chest and feel his heart beat just for her.

"Jean Paul repeatedly tells me that I am an ass, and I have finally realized that he is right."

She bit back a smile. So Jean Paul had been badgering Stefano just as he had her.

"You are lucky to have such a good friend," she said.

"So he tells me."

They shared a laugh, and the tension needling her spine eased. She still was wary, but she couldn't abide idle chit-chat with him, not when there was still so much unsaid between them.

"I'm sorry that I didn't trust you with my problems regarding Emilio," she said. "I wasn't used to sharing that burden with anyone, much less with a man who clearly disliked and disapproved of my brother."

There, she'd said it. The burden was off her now, but she still ached inside for what they'd had and lost.

He shook his head and mumbled under his breath. "Sharing. We have both failed in that regard. But that is in the past. Tell me, *bella*, are you happy? Is this where you want to be?"

"Some days I can't imagine living anywhere else."

"And others?"

"I miss the fast pace of my job. The people. The sense of being needed." She met his steady gaze. "I miss you."

Again that slow smile that made her toes curl. "Then come back to me."

She'd waited forever to hear him say that, but it wasn't enough. She needed more assurance from him. She deserved more.

She shook her head. "I can't."

"Yes, you can. And you will."

Such pride. Such arrogance. Such insight to know that was exactly what she wanted to do.

But she was afraid of trusting him. Of trusting her emotions around him. Of trusting that he'd somehow changed.

"Why should I, Stefano? Give me one good reason to return to you."

"Because we are good together." He cupped her face and

this time she leaned into it and welcomed the heat and power of the man as it sank into her. "Because you love me, *bella*." He nudged her face up and brushed a kiss over her mouth. "Because I love you."

"Do you? Or are you telling me what I want to hear?"

"It is the truth, *mio caro*. It took losing you to realize just how much I love you." His fingers twined with hers and he lifted her left hand, kissing each finger while his dark gaze adored her. "You are my sun. My reason to breathe."

"As you are mine," she said. "I love you so."

He slowly bent his head and brushed his lips against hers. "*Mio amore*."

She clutched his hand and felt his blood pounding in tandem with her own, felt tears sting her eyes. "Say it again."

"My love." He covered her mouth with his and kissed her with more heat and passion than she thought possible.

"Am I dreaming?" she asked when they pulled apart a fraction.

"No. This is real. What we feel for each other is real. I love you, Gemma Cardone. I've loved you since the first day I saw you in Marinetti Shipyard looking prim yet so desirable that you took my breath away."

There was no doubt he wanted her. But while she thrilled over the fact he loved her, she was afraid to guess what her role would be in his life.

"So you're giving me back my old job?" she asked after screwing up her courage.

"Job? No." He pulled something from his pocket and held it up. "Forgive me for not giving you this sooner."

She caught a glimpse of a gold band clutched between his long, tanned fingers. "You found my ring?"

"*Bella*! Don't you see?"

She shook her head, confused and scared to believe what was before her eyes.

He took her left hand and slid the ring on her finger. Her heart skipped a beat as she stared at the huge diamond that sparked an aura of fire to mirror the explosion of love going off inside her.

"Marry me, *bella*."

That brought her gaze flying to his. Marriage? Love? Could it all be true?

He stroked his fingers along her cheek and she shivered as much from passion as his tenderness that touched her heart. "I want you to be my wife. My partner in life. The mother of my children. I want to share everything I have with you, now and forever."

"You're sure?" she asked.

Desire blazed in his dark eyes to chase away her last remaining chill of uncertainty. He lifted her left hand and placed a kiss on each finger and his warm breath fanned flames that were already raging out of control.

"Without a doubt. Marry me, *bella*."

"Yes," she said through her tears, twining her fingers with his. "Yes."

"We can live anywhere you want. Travel anywhere you wish," he said, his eyes glittering with love. "I will arrange for your nonna to have help here as well, if she wishes."

She pressed two fingers over his perfectly sculpted lips. "Stefano, what are you doing? We are on the path of lovers. This isn't the place to waste time talking."

"No?" he asked, affecting a perfectly shocked expression that she didn't believe for a moment.

She shook her head, loving him more with each breath she took. "Kiss me," she said and lifted her mouth to his.

She didn't have to ask him twice.

So with the fragrant wild herbs scenting the air and the sea crashing on the cliffs below them, they sealed their avowal of love with all the passion in their hearts.

MILLS & BOON

JUNE 2010 HARDBACK TITLES

ROMANCE

Marriage: To Claim His Twins	Penny Jordan
The Royal Baby Revelation	Sharon Kendrick
Under the Spaniard's Lock and Key	Kim Lawrence
Sweet Surrender with the Millionaire	Helen Brooks
The Virgin's Proposition	Anne McAllister
Scandal: His Majesty's Love-Child	Annie West
Bride in a Gilded Cage	Abby Green
Innocent in the Italian's Possession	Janette Kenny
The Master of Highbridge Manor	Susanne James
The Power of the Legendary Greek	Catherine George
Miracle for the Girl Next Door	Rebecca Winters
Mother of the Bride	Caroline Anderson
What's A Housekeeper To Do?	Jennie Adams
Tipping the Waitress with Diamonds	Nina Harrington
Saving Cinderella!	Myrna Mackenzie
Their Newborn Gift	Nikki Logan
The Midwife and the Millionaire	Fiona McArthur
Knight on the Children's Ward	Carol Marinelli

HISTORICAL

Rake Beyond Redemption	Anne O'Brien
A Thoroughly Compromised Lady	Bronwyn Scott
In the Master's Bed	Blythe Gifford

MEDICAL™

From Single Mum to Lady	Judy Campbell
Children's Doctor, Shy Nurse	Molly Evans
Hawaiian Sunset, Dream Proposal	Joanna Neil
Rescued: Mother and Baby	Anne Fraser

JUNE 2010 LARGE PRINT TITLES

ROMANCE

HISTORICAL

MEDICAL™

JULY 2010 HARDBACK TITLES

ROMANCE

HISTORICAL

MEDICAL™

JULY 2010 LARGE PRINT TITLES

ROMANCE

Greek Tycoon, Inexperienced Mistress	Lynne Graham
The Master's Mistress	Carole Mortimer
The Andreou Marriage Arrangement	Helen Bianchin
Untamed Italian, Blackmailed Innocent	Jacqueline Baird
Outback Bachelor	Margaret Way
The Cattleman's Adopted Family	Barbara Hannay
Oh-So-Sensible Secretary	Jessica Hart
Housekeeper's Happy-Ever-After	Fiona Harper

HISTORICAL

One Unashamed Night	Sophia James
The Captain's Mysterious Lady	Mary Nichols
The Major and the Pickpocket	Lucy Ashford

MEDICAL™

Posh Doc, Society Wedding	Joanna Neil
The Doctor's Rebel Knight	Melanie Milburne
A Mother for the Italian's Twins	Margaret McDonagh
Their Baby Surprise	Jennifer Taylor
New Boss, New-Year Bride	Lucy Clark
Greek Doctor Claims His Bride	Margaret Barker